JUST CALL ME LADY

A Romantic Comedy By Sherry Halperin

Dedicated to my family and friends.

Yup – YOU!!!

CHAPTER ONE

I'm pathetic. No wonder I haven't had sex in four years. I stood in front of the bathroom mirror glaring at my naked image. This daily self-pity ritual had been part of my morning routine for years. I looked, I pulled, tugged and swore I would go on a diet . . . tomorrow. Always tomorrow.

My body was thick. Growing up, my mother called me *large boned*. I called myself fat. I'm five foot seven and at age twenty-nine, I had at least forty excess pounds, maybe fifty . . . protection from the cold, protection from starvation, and protection from having a life. Where was the confidence gene when I was born? That was four years ago. But life changes. My name is Constance Botello and this is how I became a Lady.

May, 2016

"So, how's your day, Connie? And I want to hear something positive for a change. I just finished this super amaaahzing Wayne Dyer book and he says, now listen closely and I quote, "*With everything that has happened to you,*

you can feel sorry for yourself or treat what has happened as a gift. Everything is either an opportunity to grow, - You listening Connie? *- Or an obstacle to keep you from growing. You get to choose.* Ahhhh, Wayne the Wonderful."

"I choose for you to zip your mouth, Peter. You're really bugging me."

I started to unpack a crate of paintings so I wouldn't have to look at my co-worker. Maybe he would stop his psychological banter and leave me to my very comfortable self-deprecation. Business was slow which made small talk way too easy. The snow birds had left Palm Desert, and the art galleries along El Paseo were mostly empty. I worked at one called California Desert Art. It was small but tastefully decorated with chocolate brown and beige suede walls, distressed concrete floors and exposed open vent ceilings. We carried works by Swinnerton, Fitch and John Hilton as well as many local artists. Class act shop. I knew I was fortunate to have a job in this industry, albeit hardly the one I had dreamed about.

Peter continued, unabashed by my terse response. "Just asking, my dear." He rounded the crate and continued, "I don't understand. You're bored with life and bored with this job, fascinating as it is. You hate your looks. What you need is a good lay. Does wonders for me. Want me to hook you up? Match.com maybe?" Peter had his hands on his hips, lecturing me as if I was his child.

I stopped unwrapping and looked up, way up, at my six-foot four-inch friend.

"You already know all the answers, but I'll humor you because I want to get the hell out of here early."

Peter smiled and sat on an empty wooden crate; legs crossed looking somewhat like a praying mantis.

I paced.

"Number one: You see that I'm stuck here all-day cataloging, authenticating and researching paintings so you get to sell them. My job ... one big yawn fest. Your job ...challenging, stimulating, social and energizing.

Number two: No one comes into the back room so I don't meet anyone new. Lonely. Isolating.

And number three: At my age, I have no idea how to meet men, so I have basically given up. The desert is a ...a...well, desert when it comes to straight men under forty. Hate online dating. Can't afford a matchmaker or that Take Me To Lunch thing. That's it. *Finito*. Please let me be miserable without all your psycho-babble."

Peter jumped up. "Sweetie, there are bars, dance clubs,

theme parties."

"I don't do bars or clubs or theme parties. I'm not gay, Peter. That's your life."

"Don't get frothy. Best friend is only trying to help."

"Peter, look at me. I'm a Red Book *before* ad. You know, the kind that sells hair removal products or the one that promises you'll *lose thirty pounds in thirty days*. I've always been the *before* and always will be."

"Stop that." Peter's voice got louder. "You're beautiful. A little rough around the edges, but still a brilliant gem. Maybe a stone that hasn't been mined yet …a naïve, pre-gem."

"You say that because you could never think of me sexually. We're buddies. Pals. Besties. Look, the truth is my ears are too small, my breasts are way too big and bottom line, my parents hated every boy I brought home when I was in high school. I learned very early on not to trust my judgment in men – or most things, for that matter. Your Connie is destined to be a fag hag for the rest of her life."

Peter frowned as he looked at me inquisitively and asked. "Why are you smirking? What's so funny?"

"I just haven't used that term before. Fag Hag. Is that P C or a no no?"

I knew I was just spouting excuses. The same ones I had told myself daily for years. My parents were dead and the excuses were getting old . . . like me.

"Peter, I know I've only been here an hour but can I have the rest of the day off? I have a paper due tomorrow. Need to do lots of research and writing which, of course, I'll make tolerable by consuming gobs of something gooey and chocolate. You can handle things here, okay?"

"Go. Eat your gooey nutritionally challenged excuse for food." Peter wrapped his long arms around me with a protective hug. "What's this one on, anyway? Anything interesting?"

"Oh, just some French dude author and some abstract artists. Nothing earth shattering." I straightened the paperwork on my cluttered desk, grabbed my lunch bag from the mini frig and walked to the back door. "Talk to you later. Call if you miraculously get slammed. I can be back here in fifteen minutes. Thanks for understanding." I paused and blew Peter a kiss. "I owe you."

"Like I have a choice?" Peter returned the air kiss. "Ciao, darling. Be a good little student. I'll hold down the fort."

Only four more credits and I'd have a master's in art

history. An online degree wasn't what I dreamed of but I had supported myself for the past eleven years and it was my only path. I would have no semesters abroad. The Sorbonne was only a dream. There would be no apprenticeships at the Uffizi or offers from Chelsea art galleries. I'm the woman stuck with big dreams and an empty wallet.

Compare the style of Nobel Prize winner Claude Simon to the artistic trends in Southern France between 1955 and 1960.

Easy does it. I'll juxtapose Simon to Picasso or Dali.

I poured myself a huge mug of decaf, got two brownies from the freezer, adjusted the back of my desk chair and settled in for seven or eight hours of tedious work.

Computer on.

Search . . . I typed in Salvador Dali and found twelve thousand, five hundred and six sites. Well, maybe not that many but a lot.

"OMG. I'll narrow it down later. Start with Simon." I was having a conversation with my computer. Sad.

Search . . . I typed in NOBLE.

"What the hell is this? Noble titles?" I looked at the computer not understanding what I had found. "You can buy a title? Yeah, right."

Why had I landed on this site? Oh, misspelled Nobel!

Corrected the spelling and started to research Claude Simon followed by Dali.

Roughly fourteen hundred words, three coffees, and four trips to the bathroom later, I finished my first draft. The writing came easy. There were no interruptions and Dali had always intrigued me. From Spanish beaches to melting clocks. Genius or insane?

I stared at my HP. *What next? Should I call Peter? No money to go shopping. Don't need anything anyway.*

Ring.

"Sweet, delicious C. . . it's Peter. No interesting men at Chino's tonight. Just the usual after work crowd of boys."

"Hi. Was just going to call you. Sorry you came up empty." I compulsively cleaned the phone with a wet napkin as I listened.

"Want to catch a movie?" Peter asked.

"Sure. Foreign or domestic?" I really didn't care. I just wanted to get out of the apartment.

"Oh, you pick, doll. Something funny, but not too romantic. Not too violent and not too deep. Anything. Call me on my cell with the theatre. I'll meet you there. Going to grab a burger."

"Let me check what's playing and I'll get back to you in ten. *Ciao.*"

"Au revoir."

"Good bye, Peter." I laughed as I put the clean phone back onto its cradle. Yes, I still had a land line.

I took the damp napkin and wiped the front of the computer. It really didn't need cleaning but I did it anyway.

MOVIES IN PALM DESERT . . .*click*. Twenty-seven films at six theatres. *What to see?* I stared at the computer wanting it to make the selection for me.

Instead, I went back to my home page and slowly typed NOBLE and Titles for Sale in the search engine. *Click*. Up sprang the web sites that had captured my imagination a few hours earlier. *Could it be possible?* Apparently so. A nobody like me, Connie Botello, could buy a noble title and become a Duchess, a Baroness or a Countess?

I read on: *This is your opportunity to join the elite of the world and be the envy of your friends, neighbors and colleagues. Our company provides you with a legal title that will effectively change your life forever. Wouldn't it be nice to get the best seats in restaurants, upgrades on planes, and invitations to the most enviable parties in town?*

Well, all you need to do is fill in this application and it can all be yours.

You may ask "How is this possible?" Well, Lady Stephanie Eugenie Parker Livingston du Exeter in Devonshire, England is allowing us to sell small parcels of her land. With this Seated Title comes the ability to pass on the land and honour to generations to come. The land is a token. But the title is genuine.

The purchase price is just fifteen hundred pounds or roughly eighteen hundred American dollars . . . a pittance for what it will provide you in esteem and recognition.

Change people's attitude toward you. Become an important person in your community. Be admired...

These are the current seated titles available as of today. Act quickly. Once they are taken, they are gone forever.

I looked up from the computer and around my small one-bedroom apartment. At twenty-nine, I was still living like a college student. Most of my furniture was picked up from thrift stores, garage sales or Craig's List. The place had no style. No class . . . only functional. How could this have happened? After all, I have a degree in art ... a subject that should demand fine taste. I had the vision, just not the bucks.

I returned to the movie list.

"Peter. It's me. How about seven o'clock at the Regal? We can see an old Woody Allen film or Phyish, a Swedish comedy about mermaids."

9

"Great. Let's see Phyish. I had the chips with dinner." Peter laughed at his attempted joke.

"Not even a little funny, Peter. See you in an hour. Love you."

I returned to the nobility site. *Eighteen hundred dollars.* But if it changed my life, if it gave me confidence and purpose, it would be worth every penny.

How could I suddenly pass myself off as nobility? It has to be legit since I would own the land. And it's all done by an English Barrister so it has to be real. Lawyers can't lie. They take some kind of truth oath.

Introducing Miss Botello, the Duchess of Wellington. *No, sounds like the main course at a steak house.* I would like you to meet Lady Botello of Cornwell. It's our pleasure to welcome Countess Connie of Berkshire. The fantasy sounded beyond exciting. The name needed some work.

"Okay, let's see what's available." I was talking to the computer again.

Click.

Lord & Lady of Middleberry	Lord & Lady of Alpont
Lord & Lady of Idenshire	Lord & Lady of Marshalle
Lord & Lady of Sacombe-on-Avon	Lord & Lady of Tickencote
Lord & Lady of Revesby-on-Avon	Lord & Lady of Ubley-on-Avon
Lord & Lady of Garsdonshire	Lord & Lady of Widford
Lord & Lady of Wookeyshire	Lord & Lady of Reephamshire
Lord & Lady of Tyberton	Lord & Lady of Yoxalle
Lord & Lady of Cropston	Lord & Lady of Blackhamsford
Lord & Lady of Dodfordshire	Lord & Lady of Jetingtoon

I read each title out loud with my name in front. "Lady Constance of Tickencote, Lady Constance of Wookeyshire. Sounds like a name out of Star Wars. Lady Constance of Widford." *Yes*, I thought. *That sounds right. Elegant without being over the top. Introducing Lady Constance of Widford.*

It would be my secret, my project. Only Peter could know. Should I spend that much money? Will a title be my panacea? My head felt like it was going to burst. I was dizzy and ran to get a drink of water from the sink. As the cool liquid drenched my throat, I looked around the space I called home, shook my head in disbelief and calmly walked back to my computer.

Click.

Name: Constance Botello

Method of payment: MasterCard

Title Requested: Lady Constance of Widford

I looked at the screen and paused.

Click.

It was done. I took in an extra deep breath, as if the air was my strength.

"YEEESSS" I screamed with enthusiasm. "I am going to be a Lady."

CHAPTER TWO

Peter was already waiting in front of the theatre when I arrived. Every inch of this lanky, flamboyant man screamed girlfriend. He wore his blond hair in a retro Caesar cut and didn't have one ounce of fat on his perfect body. Enviable.

Peter checked his watch. "You're ten minutes late. We're going to miss the previews."

"Hold on." I tugged on his arm. "Let's not see a film tonight."

"We can choose another one if you like." His voice was high, almost whining.

"No. Let's just get some coffee and talk. Can we do that? Please?"

Peter gave me a huge hug. "My baby has more problems?"

"No, just the opposite. I have an exciting project that I hope you'll help me with. It's amazing. Off the charts. But I need your advice and lots of support. Are you in?"

"Honey, if it's semi legal and doesn't cost more than

ten bucks, I'm there. To hell with the movie . . . start dishing."

As we walked to the mall Starbucks, I started to lay the ground work for Peter's role.

"You're so good at detail. And your taste is impeccable. I really, really want this to happen, Peter."

"Out with it, sister. You're driving me nuts. Want what to happen?" Peter shifted to the edge of his chair.

I continued. "Okay, I need you to make me over. You know, clothes, hair and body."

Peter looked at me, his face totally blank, and then slowly grinned from ear to ear. "I hope you mean a Eliza Doolittle makeover and not a Joan Rivers."

"Eliza . . . but not that extreme. Oh God, I'm that bad?" I was upset with the comparison but knew deep down that my friend was right and quickly continued. "Yes. I guess I do need the complete Doolittle job. I'll be the Italian Pygmalion."

"Then you're going to need more than hair and poundage, my dear." I winced at Peter's remark. He continued, "What's this for, anyway? Don't get me wrong, I'm thrilled you've gotten to this place, but why now?"

I told Peter about my online nobility purchase, emphasizing all the positive things the web site promised.

"I'm going to be a Lady."

He almost fell off his chair in excitement. "Shut up! That is too fabuloso. Never knew you could do such a thing. Sorry, continue darling."

"You're always pushing me to try something daring, out of my comfort zone. Well, I'm taking the leap. Do you think I can pull it off? It's not illegal…at least according to the web site and this barrister in England who has the connection. I buy the land and the British Lady gives me the title."

Peter knew everything about me…how I was raised, Goodwill clothes, continuous verbal abuse from my bartender father. For years, I believed Mom did her best, but as time went by, I knew my memories were sugar coated and far from reality. Mom was a drunk . . . a fall-down, loud-mouthed, throw-up-in-the-kitchen sink drunk. And, Dad was there to supply the booze and join in on daytime binges. A DUI driver was the cause of the accident that killed both of them when I was eighteen. Ironic. There were no relatives to rescue me. No insurance policies to support me. I worked two jobs waitressing and casino hosting to survive while getting a degree from the California State University in Riverside. It took me seven years, but I did it.

My interest in the visual arts was sparked by a ninth-grade school outing to the Palm Springs Art Museum. I had never seen anything like it. Modigliani's stone head sculpture; the splashes of rich hues in Frankenthaler's Carousel. Paintings that looked dimensional. Color combinations that created happy visions. From that day on, I made weekly visits to the library checking out books on the masters and twentieth century artists. I lost myself in the magnificent paintings. I escaped to Chagall's French coast and dreamt of being a Degas ballerina. Fantasy helped me tolerate my reality. The paintings expanded my horizon which in truth had only taken me a hundred miles south to San Diego. Religion was non-existent in my family, so there was no solace from a God. Mom and Dad socialized at the bar with fellow drunks, leaving me alone to create what I thought family life should be. Food soothed my soul but did not feed my ego. I was a damaged survivor.

Shortly after joining the staff at California Desert Art, Peter became my best friend, my shrink, my family and confidant. He got me and was impressed with my scholastic accomplishments, but confused by my social ineptness. My affection for funny, quirky, adorable Peter was instant and deep. That was almost five years ago.

Peter answered, "Honey, I'm over the moon. We'll call in the troops. But it won't be easy. You have resisted change for years. I'll be the General, and you'll be my little soldier. I've never seen you this excited."

I snapped back. "I don't want other people involved. We can do it . . .just the two of us. You, me . . . the General and the soldier. I don't even know where this is going."

"I can do some miracles but not everything. We need a team. They'll be supportive, I promise. Okay?"

"No, Peter. Just you and me." I was adamant.

"Sweetie. It's me. And I say we need a team. Not another word." He was more adamant.

"I'm so ready, Peter." I caved and trusted that my best friend would protect me. "How do we begin?"

Peter stroked his chin as if there were a beard to play with, took a pen out of his breast pocket and began writing on a napkin.

"Plan of attack…"

"What are you writing?" I was so scared and excited I almost choked on a chip of ice from my blended frozen mocha. I wasn't completely sure what a Noble person did or how they acted. All I was sure of was that the life of a Lady had to be more exciting than the one I had been living.

I knew I was challenged in many ways. That was no secret. But deep down, I did have dreams and a desire to be more.

"A Trainer. Oh God, I know you'll hate this, but you must have one." Peter looked up at me. "Honest my dear, it's good to sweat."

Before I could answer Peter blurted out, "Steven. He's perfect and cheap. Probably free. Have you seen his abs? To die for."

My friend's face flushed as I asked, "I didn't think he worked with women?"

"A Lady or a queen, what's the difference? He'll be great. I'll call him when I get home. Makeup." Peter looked at me again, this time for suggestions and continued.

"Your days of being au natural are over. We'll use The Boys Club on El Paseo. Tony in particular will do your makeup." Peter continued without taking a breath. "I'll do your etiquette and wardrobe styling. We'll have so much fun shopping. And Bruce, yes coiffeur extraordinaire, will do your hair. Oh, we have our own Queer Eye team . . . Steven, Tony, Bruce and me. I could just faint."

I looked at Peter and wished he wasn't gay. He loved me like no one ever had. How lucky I was to have this wonderful, weird friend.

"Thank you, Peter. I love you." I gave him a kiss on the cheek.

"Oh, stop that. I'll cry." He cleared his throat and quickly moved on. "Twelve hundred calories. That's it. No more. Starting tomorrow. I'll round up the troops. First meeting of, of …I gather it's a go?"

I nodded but doubted Peter even noticed. He thought for a moment and then, "I've got it. BALS … Becoming A Lady Society. I think that's a brilliant name for our group. We'll meet tomorrow night at my place. Seven o'clock sharp."

I nodded again as if to say, fine job, great job, holy shit it's going to happen job.

As I pushed my chair back, Peter motioned for me to stay seated. He rose, made a deep curtsy pretending to lift the side of his imaginary skirt and took my hand in his.

"Allow me, My Lady. Until tomorrow."

CHAPTER THREE

Thank goodness the tomorrow Peter spoke of was a work day. I kept busy and tried not to think about project BALS. For breakfast, my nourishment was a packet of instant oatmeal I found in the back of my kitchen cupboard. Zapped it in the microwave and added some skim milk. Disgusting, compared to the usual eggs and sausages from McDonalds I devoured every day on my way to the gallery. For lunch, I bought a tuna salad at the deli around the corner and drizzled some balsamic vinegar over it.

The day was mercifully busy. A new shipment of watercolors came in, and I spent hours cataloging them on the computer. Periodically I joined Peter in the main showroom where he refused to discuss what strategy BALS was formulating. All I knew was that the boys were in.

Apple slices abated the jitters around four. Dinner was catered by Healthy Choice.

My stomach was growling. I was miserable and desperately wanted an In N Out double burger with special fries and chili. Actually, I drove by one on the way to Peter's, parked and inhaled the delicious aroma.

Peter's Rancho Mirage condo was about three miles from my apartment. This small city is one of seven that make up the beautiful Coachella Valley of California. His parents had given him the down payment, probably as forgiveness money for not speaking to him the entire year he *came out*. Now, they're a close family. Mrs. Barker even scouts potential boyfriends for her son. She means well, but infuriates Peter every time she calls with a phone number. The condo was mid-century modern, done in oranges, pinks and browns. With the chocolate shag rug and the chrome kitchen table with fuchsia and beige plaid seats, his place was a cross between an early James Bond film and The Brady Bunch home.

When I arrived at seven, all four men were seated in the living room, drinking Cosmopolitans and munching on peanut butter filled pretzels. They rose in unison when I entered, each playfully curtsying or bowing, alerting me that Peter had already let them in on my project.

Bruce, the Hair man, approached with a gentle hug which quickly exploded into overzealous enthusiasm while he scrunched my hair. "Just look at this. A thick mop. The only way to describe it, right? Ugh, Jewish and Italian hair! Glad I'm British." He kept running his fingers through my mane as Tony, the dark, handsome, Sephardic makeup man, stood two inches from my face analyzing my pores, nose and eyes. Meanwhile, Steven the trainer, approached me from the back and gave my ass a feel.

"Whoa!" I yelped as I lunged forward.

"Boys, sit." The General spoke.

"We're all just excited." Tony squealed as they went back to the couch.

Peter poured me a Cosmo. "Here, your last drink for the next four months." He took off one of his size fourteen shoes and banged it on the coffee table. Peter, the dramatic one… "I hereby call the first meeting of BALS to order. I've laid out our strategic plan. But, before we get started Connie, we have a gift for you."

"You guys. You didn't have to buy me anything. Your help is more than enough."

"Well," Bruce the hairdresser chimed in, "We didn't exactly go shopping for this. When Peter told us about your project, it really touched our hearts. New beginnings are so special. And we know how much you've struggled with years of back aches and those deep ridges in your shoulders. Ouch.

So, Tony, Peter, Steven and I got on a conference call with David Letters. Dr. David Letters." Bruce stood, moved to the coffee table in front of me, sat down on it and took my hands in his. He looked like a cross between Don Knotts and Niles from that Frasier show. "And guess what, he's going to do your boob job for free. And we're picking up the tab for the outpatient clinic."

I sat there speechless. My first thoughts were, *What's in it for them?* And, who told them I even wanted a breast reduction? Then I remembered who I was dealing with. . . four men who all wanted to be mothers. "I can't accept that. But thank you so much."

"What do you mean?" Bruce tittered excitedly. "He owes me. I've been schtupping the good doctor for the past three years. We'd be married if he didn't insist on that damn prenup." We all laughed. "You'll have the reduction, and we'll take care of you. *Fini*!" Bruce was resolute.

I began to tear up and felt my face heat up, surely turning red. I knew I could lose the weight, or at least give it a good try - but the boob job? There was no way I could afford that. Every cent I had was used for necessities. The girls hung low and at a cup size E or F, they were a mental and physical problem.

"Of course," Bruce continued, "he'll have to examine you and confirm you're a candidate, which of course you will be. Just look at those bazongas. Triple D's, E's? Oh honey, what your poor back has held up all these years."

I sat silent.

Peter fanned his face with a copy of European Bazaar. "Sweetie, put a smile on that face. Or else you'll have all of us bawling with you".

"And another thing," Bruce continued enthusiastically, "you'll need a new place to locate and a new job. You can't stay here in the desert. Too many people know you. I have a cousin, Phil, in Bev Hills whose close friend, a Mr. Rothstein, does private art purchases for very wealthy people. He's kind of a decorator but instead of wallpaper, he uses a Matisse or Picasso. This Rothstein guy was very impressed with your title and the degrees I made up. Phil called him this morning. He'll give you a job if you want. Said you can start in the Fall. Peter helped me with your resume. Of course, we faked quite a bit but hell, everyone does."

The hair guru stopped to sip his cosmo then continued.

"You have to call him in a month to discuss salary . . . when you get back from England and your visit with Auntie

Clementine."

I looked at Bruce and he winked back. "Aunt Clementine?" And then I caught on. "Oh, yes, of course, my Auntie in England." I hadn't thought that far ahead, but I would need to move where nobody knew me and find some way to support myself. My emotions were all over the chart. I was excited, but I was also nervous and scared. What would it be like to enter a new world of friends and business associates based on lies? No, I stopped my negative thoughts. Not lies. The title is real. I own the land. I've never been a liar. Hell, I was a Girl Scout.

"Peter, I have to move?" I looked at him as if this realization was a death sentence. "Of course, I have to move. But I can't be away from you. You're my family."

Peter put a finger to his lips to shush me. "We'll talk about that later."

"Okay, here's the game plan." Peter continued with renewed energy. "Steven, trainer extraordinaire, you start work tomorrow, six in the morning.

Can you make it three times a week?"

"Of course, my dear. Anything for the cause. Connie, get ready to work your ass off . . . literally."

Peter sat down next to Bruce. "Want you to do a trial

run in a month or so. Final color and cut won't be until the end of the summer.

"Gotcha." Bruce replied. "Connie, I'll be in touch and work out the day and time."

Tony raised his hand. "What about me? What about me?"

Peter explained that makeup lessons wouldn't start until after the surgery and before the final haircut.

"But Tony, I would love you to help me with style, etiquette and history." Peter was flirting with the handsome Boys Club hunk. "I'll start brushing up on which fork goes next to what. Connie was never taught any social graces, let alone exposed to true etiquette. Bone up on British history. Meanwhile, Connie, start walking with a book on your head – great for posture. The first official meeting of BALS is over. Let's have another Cosmo." Then he looked me square in the eyes, "Sparkling water for you, my Lady."

I was overwhelmed. I was also a bit tipsy from the one Cosmo I drank earlier. Alcohol was not something I enjoyed or indulged in very often. Past history had shown me its demons. Tony put a Best of '60's Disco CD on and took Peter's hand to dance. Steven pulled me off the couch and twirled me like a top.

"Great exercise, honey. Swing those arms. Move those hips." My trainer was already working.

Peter and Bruce chimed in. "That's it. Shake it baby. You can do it."

I was on my way to a new life, a new me. With BALS in tow, we would be the girls of summer.

CHAPTER FOUR

T rainer Steven looked almost square. His upper body muscles were so huge and he was so short, that with his blonde crew cut he was the human version of Sponge Bob.

"And one and two and three and … "

Every inch of my body begged to stop this foreign abuse. But drill

sergeant Steven kept me marching along, singing Donna Summer disco hits like they were Marine Corp hymns.

"*She works hard for her money. Yeah. Yeah. She works hard for her money. Yeah, yeah.*"

It was impossible not to catch Steven's enthusiasm and I soon started to sing my own rendition of *Let's Dance* as I walked along the palm tree lined street in front of my apartment.

"Come on Steven, sing. I've caught your boogielishous enthusiasm." I was amazed at my attitude …and switched to singing *These Boots Were Made For Walking*. Despite the pain, I began skipping along with my new buddy … at six in the morning, a time of day that was totally alien to me. I even caught myself smiling. But by mile one, my happy face was gone and by mile two, I was grimacing. My legs were shaking like they were snapped rubber bands. So out of shape.

Crippled over and holding my stomach, I managed to take in enough oxygen to get out a few words. "Can't do this, Steven. I'm dying here."

"No pity. Anyway, you're almost home, and we're done for today. Take a hot shower and some Tylenol. I expect you to climb your apartment stairs six times tomorrow, walk two miles and do thirty sit ups. See you Thursday. *Ciao*, baby. I'm off to rub some bodies."

"Excuse me?" My words stopped Steven at his red Mustang convertible.

"Don't plotz. I'm a part-time massage therapist at the Marriott. *Ciao for now.*"

By the time I arrived at work, my muscles were visibly pulsing, and I was walking like an old man with major hemorrhoids. Even though I had parked in the delivery zone right next to the back door, the few steps necessary to enter the gallery were excruciating.

"Connie, what the hell is wrong with you?" Peter helped me onto a cushioned seat in the back room.

"I'll be fine. Steven promised. But right now, I want to dip him in flour and sauté him in pig fat."

Workout two with my Nazi-like trainer was a mixture of aerobics and medicine ball play. Workout three added bar bells and a jump rope. Four was power walking and five added weights while I marched around the park. Steven was tough. He didn't tolerate complaining and called me a wuss every time I stopped to catch my breath. We climbed the beautiful Bump and Grind trail of the Valley's San Jacinto Mountains and used the flat Palm Desert community park as our gym. The early morning sunlight was beautiful on the desert floor. Colors seemed heightened and the air was cool and fresh . . .a pleasant welcome to the century mark temps that would be delivered later in the day.

And so, my change began. I even bought a Wayne Dyer book at Barnes & Noble: Change Your Thoughts – Change Your Life.

As time passed, I could tell I was shedding pounds but was afraid to get on the scale. Not that I was allowed. Once a week. No more, were my orders from Peter.

By day thirty, the results were in. I had lost nine pounds and celebrated with the boys of BALS by having a non-fat chocolate frozen yogurt. It was cool, creamy and tasted like I was really cheating.

"Shoulders back. Head high. Now glide, don't lumber." Peter ordered while ever-so-handsome Tony squeezed my shoulders together from the back. It was Sunday and my apartment was transformed into a studio for the societally challenged. The couch was pushed against the wall to give us more walking space and the old matted green living room rug, acquired free from an old lady in my building who went into a nursing home, was rolled up and hauled into the kitchen.

"Ouch. I can't pull them back any farther. My huge twins force me forward."

Peter came over, took his belt off and tied my wrists together behind my back. "I know you must think this is kinky…"

Tony interrupted. "And it's not? " He winked at the General.

Peter gave Tony a playful, pain in the ass look. "May I please continue? Your hands behind you will thrust your chest forward and your shoulders back. Good posture comes with good breeding. Now walk. Your 'twins' will have their day soon."

Our *Miss Manners* meetings took place once a week. Peter coached me on the physical level …like leg crossing which was never over the knee but one ankle crossed behind the other and on the art of shaking hands… firm without lingering. I never realized body mechanics mimicked breeding. There was so much I didn't know. My exposure was to drunken vomit and blackened eyes, deeds that were accomplished with calloused knees and bar room brawls.

Tony took over when it came to table settings, word pronunciation, people in the news I should be aware of, and travel hot spots … basically all areas of decorum and worldliness.

We moved into the kitchen and sat around my white melamine garage sale table. Peter poured three glasses of California merlot. "Here's to the God of grapes. Chin Chin."

Tony chimed in. "When lifting a wine glass, hold it only by the stem."

"Why? It's so much easier to grab it up here." I reached for the middle of the glass.

"Sweetie, if you hold it that way, you warm the wine or

bubbly. And don't stick out that pinkie."

I tried to follow Tony's instructions but when I took what I considered a normal gulp of the red vino my instructor looked at me in horror.

"Only small sips. Glory be to Cher. You have so much to learn. Caress the liquid in your mouth and swirl it around to taste the subtleties of the grape before you swallow. I know this is cheap wine but pretend it's a Chateau Rothschild."

I wondered how this makeup man knew so much about grace and etiquette. Later, Peter told me that Tony came from means … boarding school, cotillion, country club, and was related on his Father's side to the Revlon dynasty. This dark-haired god of a man exuded class. No wonder Peter was enamored with him. I could be, too.

About week six, little Bruce weighed in on the hair.

"It is too long and drab. Let's do a cut first. See how it flows. After, we'll decide on color."

I was sitting in his empty salon on El Paseo, the Rodeo Drive of Palm Desert. It was hardly a traditional beauty parlor, more like the living room of a very wealthy woman with extremely over-the-top taste. Perhaps the decorator had visited a bordello. Almost everything was gilded and oversized which made my hairdresser seem even smaller than he was. There were five cutting stations, each separated from the other by a curtain of red satin that flowed from the ceiling to the floor.

Peter held my hand as Bruce clipped away. "Not too short, Bruce," I said. "I've never had short hair. It's not me." Why was I so attached to my mane? I knew it would grow back, but I was still terrified.

"Shhhhh. Remember, dearie, we're going for a new look. Gorgeous Barry Manilow lets me do his do... so I can do you. Ha! I rhymed. Give her a stiff drink, Peter."

Instead, I was handed a Diet Snapple in a stemmed wine glass and was complimented on my perfect fluted goblet hold.

"Oh, my girl is doing so well. Just look at her, Bruce. From butch to beautiful." Peter beamed with pride.

"Finished." With a flurry, Bruce swirled off the plastic cape and slowly turned the chair so I could see my new cut in the mirror.

I was shocked at first. He had clipped at least six inches off. My hair was now a little above my shoulders, cut blunt, and very chic. Bruce had tucked the front hairs behind my ears and left wisps of long bangs over my right eye.

"I think I love it. Do you? Is it right? Is it …" I was stammering.

"Slow down, cowgirl." Peter studied me from every angle and finally concluded that the cut was perfect. Hugs of gratitude all around.

By week six, I had lost twelve pounds, could run/walk three miles, cross from one side of my apartment to the other without dropping the book on my head and had started to bleach my dingy teeth.

And without great fanfare, a package arrived from England with my land deed, my noble crest and documentation that I was indeed Lady Widford.

Time for the boob job!

CHAPTER FIVE

"Wake up, Connie. It's over. Wake up, sweetie. You did just fine." A nurse was talking to me in a low, soothing voice.

My teeth were chattering. I felt nauseous. "I'm so cold."

"I'll get another warmed blanket. It's normal after surgery ... the anesthetic. Just rest. Take deep breathes. The grogginess will go away soon." The nurse's voice was not reassuring.

Through my blurry eyes, the recovery room looked and felt like it was filled with snow. The clang of instruments against metal trays sounded like an explosion. I was dizzy and freezing, nauseous and scared. But it was over and I was alive.

"Nurse! Nurse! A bag ... bucket. Hurry." I hurled.

Within an hour I was wheeled out of recovery and taken to a lovely, private room where my four heroes were waiting.

"There's our girl." Peter grinned with one of his phony,

Cheshire smiles. "It wasn't so bad, was it?"

"Right now, I want to strangle you. Ask me again in a few days."

The nurse adjusted my IV and told the fab four to let me rest for a few hours. I vaguely remember Steven fluffing my pillow and Peter holding my hand.

"Our poor Connie. She looks so helpless." Tony spoke softly as he stood at the foot of the bed.

"Hey, I can hear you. Helpless, my ass. I'm just going to close my eyes for a minute and ..." I dozed off.

The dream was so vivid. I was running up and down the aisles of Victoria Secret, dancing between the round table displays of the infamous lingerie store wearing only a lace thong.

I kept looking at all the bras, totally confused. They were all red ...the color of passion. I picked up a racy number and pressed it to my breasts. It felt smooth and cool, like raspberry sorbet on a hot day in the desert.

No more Playtex. Silk, sexy. Silk, satin, sexy. Red.

I had slept for four hours and awoke with my hands stroking my bandaged breasts. As I open my eyes, I could make out three of the boys playing cards and the other reading. I was still a bit groggy.

"So, you guys were just hanging, watching me snore and drool?"

"No, no, my dear." Steven produced a bag from next to his seat and continued. "We took a little trip over to the mall.

"Enjoy." Peter chimed in as Steven handed me a bag.

"What am I going to do with you guys? Another present?" I opened the Macy's bag to find a Playtex 16 hour sports bra. "It's ..."

Peter brushed my hair back and gave me a peck on the cheek. "It's what the good doc ordered for your recovery. I know it's not sexy but Victoria is only a few weeks away. Come on, boys. Lady Constance needs more beauty rest. I'll be back in a few hours with my chariot to take you home."

After herding the other three to the door, Peter stopped, grinned and said, "And it will be red, my dear. Fire engine red. Tomato sauce, spicy salsa red. Now go to sleep, hot mama."

"Thanks, Peter. You know...for everything. I will be hot, won't I?"

Peter licked his finger, touched his ass and hissed like a

steak freshly thrown on a grill. "Sizzling. I love ya, Connie. Now get some rest."

CHAPTER SIX

I spent the following week at home recuperating, devouring lifestyle books, gleaning the finer subtleties of noble etiquette. Emily Post, Leticia Baldridge's New Manners for New Times and Lady Lupin's Book of Etiquette became my Bibles. Between chapters, I tried on every blouse, sweater and dress I owned to admire how they looked with my new breasts. They were a perfect C.

Marvelous, darling. They look absolutely divine. I mimicked Peter, as I pranced in front of the full-length mirror, the one I use to avoid. The breast job was a major consideration. I justified it as a medical need to alleviate my back and shoulder pain but truthfully, it was more my ego. Vogue and Town and Country were the unrealistic standards I looked to. Before the surgery, I could have been a pin up for Southern Farmer Gazette. Now, I was inching toward Palm Springs Life. A smidgeon of self-confidence had entered my psyche and this new feeling of self-worth felt great.

I gave written notice to my apartment manager. August thirtieth would be my last day in the desert.

The week before my surgery, the job offer in Los Angeles had come through. I found an affordable studio apartment in "Beverly Hills adjacent" that was even smaller than my desert home. It had security, a laundry room in the building and underground parking which I was told is a premium in Los Angeles. The estate of Lady Constance would be one room, a closet and bath.

Emotions waffled between wondering if I was proliferating a fraud, to embracing an exciting new life. Could I do it? Would the benefits outweigh the risks? I could call the whole thing off and many times I really considered doing just that. My job at California Desert Art was secure. Peter would always let me stay.

I own land in England and my title is real. That was my mantra and I was sticking to it. My new life was going to be wonderful.

Peter took a huge gulp of raspberry iced tea. "When?"

"Not until the beginning of September." I said trying to reassure my friend.

A blond waiter approached and asked if we were ready to order. "Nothing for me." Peter snapped. I ordered a California Pizza Kitchen chopped salad. "Half portion. Dressing on the side, please."

The restaurant was crowded with chatty luncheon customers. Every booth was filled.

Peter continued to stare silently, so I talked. "We have the rest of the summer together. And then, you'll come up on your days off, and we'll go to No Ho and Boys Town and eat at Nobu and go dancing at Waste. We'll have a blast. Come on, Peter, L.A. is only two hours away. Not another continent."

Peter was noticeably disturbed. His hand shook as he picked up his iced tea. "Shit." He had bumped his glass against the napkin holder and spilled half on the table.

Again, there was an awkward silence as I cleaned up the tea and searched for words to assure my friend our closeness would continue.

"You knew I'd be moving. You were all for this adventure a few months ago. You encouraged me. You helped me with every aspect. What changed?"

"I'm sorry. I just hate the thought of losing my best friend. You've become the Connie I knew was always hidden inside that mousy facade. Your insides were always beautiful, but sorry, your outsides were in need of some fixing. Just do me one favor."

"Anything, Peter." I was thinking he was going to ask

for a picture or a daily phone call.

"Just make sure when you get my sofa bed it's extra long? You know how I hate to have my footsies dangle over the edges."

We both laughed. Peter took my hand and continued.

"Connie, I only want the best for you. Best Friend loves you. And if this move and new life is what you want, then it's a journey well deserved."

The rest of the summer whizzed by. I lost twelve more pounds, had hair man Bruce do a final styling and color. Spare time was spent packing what few books, pots and pans, glasses and pictures I owned in boxes scrounged from alleys behind the El Paseo shops and nearby grocery stores. I saved every penny and got my bank account up to a little over six thousand dollars. This would supplement my salary and allow me to indulge in manicures, eyebrow waxes and other personal maintenance rituals, mandatory and expected of a woman with a noble pedigree.

And to my amazement, I finished my Master's degree. Mama and Pop would have been proud. Well, maybe that's another dream.

But the best news was that Peter and makeup man Tony started to date. Peter was on cloud nine and Tony acted like a teenager in love. To see them holding hands at the movies and walking arm and arm as we shopped along Indian Canyon in Palm Springs filled my heart with hope of finding a love of my own.

The background story I created was that my father was British nobility and met my American mother while she was studying theatre at the London Conservatory of Drama. He was an investor and backed London and Broadway plays. I have no British accent because my first five years were spent mostly in the States while Daddy mounted several productions. Of course, summers were spent at our Baronial estate near St. George outside London. I had a pony named Chester and a nanny named Matilda. I have dual citizenship and went to Mrs. Potts boarding school in Connecticut for my elementary education. I continued my secondary schooling at Mill Hill School in London. I would proudly display on my office desk a picture I found at an antique shop of twelve uniformed prep school girls in front of an ivy walled building – my flat sisters, if anyone asked.

And so began the life I had bought for eighteen hundred dollars.

Peter and I spent our off hours hounding consignment shops for appropriate clothes, jewelry and purses. It was so much fun. July and August are great times to bargain hunt in the desert. The snow birds are gone, the heat is up and the shops need revenue.

"This looks like a Chanel, doesn't it?" Peter grabbed a navy suit off a rack in After Delights. "Look at the buttons, Connie. It's a knock off, but you'd have to be an uber fashionista to know. Try it on. Size 8. Perfect. And here, try these navy shoes."

When I emerged from the dressing room, Peter and the saleslady were all smiles. I had put my hair up with bobby pins from my purse. A few wisps trailed down my neck. My makeup was done to perfection thanks to Tony's weeks of counseling and the three-inch heels Peter had handed me were neither fuck me pumps nor butch business. They emphasized the curve of my calves perfectly and gave me an aura of strength from my toes to my French twist.

Peter took my hand and twirled me around several times admiring what he considered his creation. Suddenly, tears filled my eyes. They were tears of happiness and promise. They were also tears of fear and doubt.

Connie Botello was gone. Lady Constance had arrived.

CHAPTER SEVEN

My L.A. third floor studio apartment was only about 750 square feet and cost $2900 a month. I bought a new green sofa bed at Macy's on sale to sleep on and brought my melamine kitchen set from the desert. A bookcase, six drawer oak dresser and a few assorted knick knacks rounded out the furniture and décor of my new home.

"Peter, you'll have to sleep on a blow up. Sorry big guy. Yeah, we'll talk tomorrow. Love ya." I put down the phone, grabbed a handful of carrots and did my final arranging.

Picture of Best Friend went on the kitchen counter, next to one of Mom, Pop and me taken at my high school graduation. It was our last family picture. Every night since their death I've talked to it, held it close to my heart and most evenings, kissed the portrait hoping they could feel my love and sadness. No matter how dysfunctional, they were still my Mom and Pop.

A group shot of the BALS team about six weeks into my make over went next to the sofa on a small end table.

There were only a few pieces of art to hang; prints that I bought at street fairs.

***

Albert Rothstein, my new boss, only knew that I was Bruce's friend, and had a title through my families' lineage. The offices of Private Collectors, LTD were on Canon, about five doors north of Wilshire Blvd. in the heart of the real Beverly Hills. They were right off the elevator on the second floor and decorated by Albert's wife, Nina, in an Italian modern motif. Six sconces adorned the reception room walls with a trumpe l'oeil of angels on the ceiling. The chairs were burgundy brocade with gold tassels dangling from the arms and were separated by a glass top table with gold leaf carved legs. Finishing the overly ostentatious room was a running water fountain of cherubs in one corner and potpourri in a large bowl on the reception desk. The room smelled like my grandmother's lingerie drawer.

I was told during my phone interview that very few clients ever come to the offices but that we, as advisors and purchasing agents, went wherever they wanted us to meet. That was great news since I thought the offices were hideous.

Five of us shared the space; Mr. Rothstein, his son, Joshua, who was the head buyer and closing in on forty; the other consultant Juliet Twibble, thirty-five'ish and Mary, the twenty something receptionist/phone gal.

The first thing I noticed walking into my boss's office was a large portrait behind his desk. It was of Mr. Rothstein standing next to a black Bentley circa 1998. A plaque was attached to the frame that said: *He with the most toys wins.* That told me a lot about the man I was now working for and why he wanted someone in his office with a title. My college minor in psychology suggested that he had a large ego, was a man not to cross and probably has several rooms at his mother's nursing home named after him.

Rothstein had a good reputation according to Google and some art dealers I questioned back in the desert. This successful, confident, mustached man knew his stuff despite the fact he looked like a relative of Danny DeVito and wore a very bad toupee.

On his desk were four pictures of I assumed his wife and grandchildren. His long haired shar pei, Duke, sat at his master's right, drool hanging from his mouth. The reality I was staring at was nothing like what I had imagined for my new job. Where's the Beverly Hills sophistication? Where's the smell of wealth and glamour?

"What do I call you? Lady Constance? Madame? Your

grace?" Rothstein asked as he stood to greet me.

"Just Constance, Mr. Rothstein." The words seem to catch in my throat after hearing him refer to me as a Lady.

"Then you call me Al. Okay?" I leaned across the desk as he shook my hand, and then sat in the blue leather tufted chair.

Posture perfectly vertical? Check. *Legs crossed correctly?* Check. I passed my own internal inspection of my external self

"Welcome to our family." He continued. "First time I've met a real noble. Jews don't have relatives that are Ladies or Lords. Guess that's why we give our dogs names like Princess, Duke, Queenie." His belly shook as he chuckled. Forty-pound Duke jumped up on his lap to give him copious licks.

I smiled politely at his joke. "And I thank you, Mr. Roth… Al, for this opportunity. I'll work hard. It's been a long-time dream of mine to represent important works of art."

"Your title is going to be put to good use at PC Ltd. Get down Duke." The dog reluctantly jumped off his master and wandered over to his water dish for a few noisy laps. Rothstein continued, "We deal with the very wealthy. Worldwide clients. And, they love to name drop. At least that's what I'm counting on. So, we will be dropping Lady Constance all over town."

I looked at Al as he put out his six-inch illegal Cuban and was happily surprised at his honesty. Then why was my stomach churning and little beads of sweat appearing on my forehead? What if he did a search on my investor father? I would just say that he was behind the scenes and hated publicity – hence, no results. And my British residence? The picture I would proudly display on my desk was of a country estate hotel call Stapleford, not where I grew up. What if the Rothsteins had stayed there? *Dropping Lady Constance all over town?* Oh, God, what had I gotten myself in to?

"Gotta run over to Saks, Connie. Then, a business lunch at Spago with that Williams lady. You know the one who just inherited a fortune from her stepmother after she was killed by a falling tree." Rothstein crossed from his desk to a table with a humidor on it. "Can't be without my after lunch treat." He put a large cigar in his breast pocket and continued talking. "We close between noon and one thirty every day. Why don't you grab lunch with Mary? She can fill you in on some of our clients." He cocked his head. "And between you and me, she could use some company … always eats alone. A bit strange, but a great secretary."

"Would you like me to stay with Duke?" I offered.

"Oh no, he goes everywhere with me. Had him declared a service dog. By my side all the time. Calms my nerves. Duke, let's go. Bet Uncle Wolfgang has a special treat for my doggie woggie."

The slightly overweight receptionist and I walked a few blocks to Nate and Al's, a famous Deli on Beverly Drive where lots of stars and wanna be stars hang out. I don't think Mary said two words to me the entire way. Her stride was purposeful as her pleather purse, which was slung over her shoulder and across her chest, bounced with every step.

The wait was only ten minutes which gave me enough time to notice Sandra Bullock in a back booth with another woman and Suzanne Somers holding court at her table up front. In no time, we were seated.

"The old Rothstein is a pussy cat but the young one, watch out." Mary now seemed eager to start dishing. "He'll cut you to pieces to steal a client. He's gay, you know. Didn't figure it out until after he married the gal his mother chose for him. They have two kids. Crushed Mrs. Rothstein, Senior. Utterly crushed her. The wife wasn't too happy either."

A waitress who looked and sounded just like Shelley

Winters came to our table. "So, what's it gonna be today?" She had a perfect Bronx accent and was standing with both hands on her hips looking like the stereotypic New York Deli server."

"I'll have a cobb salad, ranch on the side, no bacon."

"Doll, this is a deli, not a spa. How about a pastrami on rye?"

I looked at the menu quickly and ordered blintzes and an iced tea. Mary had the pastrami with chopped liver and slaw and a diet Dr. Pepper.

Mary continued as the waitress blew a huge bubble with her gum and stuck the order pencil back in her hair.

"And Twibble . . . a shark. She's all nice and sweet and genteel on the outside, but sister, she's out to get every commission check she can smell. She'll do anything to land a sale, and I do mean anything." Mary laughed as she winked at me.

"Once she flew in a baby penguin from the Artic because a client's young son liked that kid's movie Happy Feet. Of course, it had to fly on a private jet and we had to pay for all the water damage the leaky ice tank caused. Senior Rothstein was furious but she landed a four-million-dollar sale."

"And what about you, Mary?" What was her past, I wondered?

"I'm boring as hell. I knit, have a cat, live in Culver City with a roommate and haven't been further east than Vegas. We should go some time. I think Circus Circus still has a $2.95 shrimp cocktail. But then, Ladies probably don't eat cheap shrimp cocktails or stay at bargain hotels." Mary looked suspiciously at me. At least I thought so. I had no answer.

This was my new life. Everyone I met that first day had agendas that could ultimately affect me if I wasn't careful. I had made my proverbial bed with the Rothsteins, Twibble and Mary. I just hoped none of them expected me to sleep in theirs.

My office was small with a desk and two blue guest chairs. Very utilitarian. At least it had a window where I could look out to Wilshire Boulevard and see some sky. On the walls were a Matisse and Rembrandt sketch. They looked real or were incredibly good imposters. A computer, phone and vase with a real yellow carnation in it completed my new work space.

About ten minutes after returning from lunch, I heard Mr. Rothstein through the intercom system. "In here,

Constance." I went down the hall. "Had an interesting phone call just now from Brazilian billionaire Estefan Safra. Made his fortune in wireless communications. You know, cell phones, cell towers and I think TV stations."

Get to the point, Rothstein. Where do I fit in?

"Anyway, he has a new 173-foot yacht temporarily moored in Marina Del Rey. They need art. Four o'clock. You'll meet with his assistant. Not sure of his name. You're perfect for this. And Connie…"

Mr. Rothstein handed me a sheet of paper, waved me off but then continued to talk which made me turn and ask, "Yes, sir?"

"Charm this guy's pants off and get that fucker to buy some serious art."

CHAPTER EIGHT

I t had been my dream to sell important art to those who would appreciate owning what only a few could afford. But as I headed to the marina in my newly leased white BMW 3, I was a nervous wreck. The "what if's" consumed me, sending shakes to my teeth and knees.

I'm a Lady from a noble family. Daddy lived in London, Mommy was American. They both are deceased. I know how to walk across a room with a book on my head. SHUT UP. I was trying to scare my thoughts away just as a red jeep laid on its horn and almost cut me off. I was back in reality.

"Peter," I had dialed my cell. "Hi, I'm on my way to my first consult. I can hardly breathe."

Peter's voice was calming. "You know what you're doing. Just be your marvelous self. Okay? Where are you meeting her?"

"It's a him and I'm headed to this huge boat in Marina Del Rey."

"How huge?" Peter asked.

"One hundred seventy - three feet."

"Yacht, Connie. It's a friggin mega yacht."

I continued. "How much is something like that worth?"

Peter put me on hold and did a quick computer search. "Well, it's worth between thirty and fifty million according to Yachting World. The owner is loaded. Call me after, sweetie. Oh, what did you have for lunch?"

"Blintzes, a side salad and tea."

"Remember to check your teeth at the next red light for any leftover green things. Ciao, I have a customer. Gotta go." Peter hung up.

In front of me was a mass of shiny white fiberglass. The yacht's name, Rico, was emblazoned across the stern which had two sets of curved stairways leading to the aft deck. As I approached in my three-inch heels, a young man wearing a body-hugging navy tee shirt and white slacks took my hand and helped me aboard.

"Please remove high shoes," he said with a slight smile and a sexy South American accent. "Here's some slippers."

"Of course. Sorry. I didn't have time to get my flats. And you are?"

"You're Lady Widford? You call me Tony, short for Antonio. Antonio Safra. This is my father's yacht."

"Please call me Constance. What a magnificent vessel.

Have you had it long?"

The young, dark haired Latin man guided me toward the main cabin and offered a glass of Fume Blanc, never answering my question. Of course, they didn't have it long. It's brand new. His hair was slicked back. Light blue eyes, a ruddy, tan complexion and strong facial bone structure made him irresistibly handsome. I couldn't believe Connie Botello was on a yacht doing business with, please God let him be single, one of the most eligible men in the world. And this was my first assignment. My hands were shaking so badly I had to hide them in the pockets of my slacks.

"No thank you, I'm working." I secretly wanted to drink the wine, tear off his clothes and screw his delicious body until he cried for me to stop. Instead, I wandered around the salon and took in the magnificence of it all. The space was multiple times larger than my entire apartment. It had a baby grand in one corner and several areas for seating. Most of the furniture was contemporary and upholstered in either tan or white leather. The bar was forward with six brown and white horse hair covered stools. "So, I see there are empty walls just waiting for some beautiful art. Do you or your father or your wife have a favorite style or artist?"

For the next hour, Antonio and I discussed possibilities

of what masters and haute current painters could adorn the main cabin, master suite, the three guest cabins, gym and hallways. Actually, I did the talking and suggesting. Antonio smiled exposing his beautiful, straight white teeth. "With the sleek lines of the ship and contemporary furniture, you are able to go in many directions. It all depends on what atmosphere you want to create." Antonio just nodded as I continued. "The art pieces you select will play a significant role in the overall style of the yacht and comfort of those onboard."

"Constance. Pieces will be selected by you and Mr. Safra . . .my father. I'm just here to show you yacht and welcome you to RICO. You know what it means, yes?"

I shook my head that I didn't.

"It means Rich. Good name, right?"

I couldn't stop starring at this Latin God. He was right out of a Ralph Lauren photo shoot. But was he single?

"Constance," We were now on the bridge overlooking the marina. "Constance, I'd like to continue talk over dinner. Tonight, yes?"

"Actually, I have plans. May I call you tomorrow with some ideas of pieces that are available?" I didn't have plans. I was going home to water my plants and play solitaire on the computer. This was all too sudden. "Antonio, do you have a budget for the art?" Again, this young Onassis didn't answer.

I picked up my shoes and headed down the aft stairway toward the dock. "Ahhhh Yikes." I tripped on the last step. Antonio rushed to my side, saving me from a sure fall in the ocean.

"Gotcha. You're okay?" He had both arms around my waist, holding me tightly.

"I'm fine. Thank you. That would have been very embarrassing."

"De nada. You safe now. Oh, and your question? There is no budget that I know of, Lady Constance." He looked me in the eyes. "Just the desire to have the best. Please email your suggestions to my father. You have his contact, right?"

"Right. Yes. I'm sure my boss does." I answered as I stared into those dreamy blue eyes.

Once Antonio was sure I was stable, he released his hold. "Tomorrow night dinner. Yes? Here's my cell number. And please, call me Tony. It's better." He slipped a piece of scrap paper into my blouse pocket. "In the afternoon is best time."

I put on one shoe and started to walk away, leaving my other behind. It was like a ghastly scene in a terrible rom com.

"You are Cinderella, yes?" The young man was a prince.

CHAPTER NINE

"So, start dishing. Tell me everything." Peter had unexpectedly come up from the desert for his first visit and we were having dinner at an Indian restaurant on Melrose.

"Where do I start? It's all amazing. He's amazing. My first few days in L.A. and I've already met a bizillionaire."

"You don't know anything about this man. Looks and money aren't everything. It's a good start, but you've known him, what, three hours?" Peter was devouring his nan and Palak Paneer.

I laughed. "Well, from this gal's point of view, it certainly was a great introduction to L.A."

Peter filled me in on the entire BALS group and local desert gossip. "We all miss you, Connie. Cosmo night at BLEND is just not the same without our girlfriend."

"I miss everyone, too. But I'm living my dream."

Peter nodded that he understood.

After dinner we walked the uber chic street. "We're not in the desert any more, sweetie. This place is just too amaaaahzing." Peter couldn't contain his enthusiasm and dragged me into every shop for blocks. I bought some wonderful strappy sandals and Peter bought two shirts. Coffee and more talk, the evening flew by.

"I want you to be careful. Take it slow. Concentrate on your job and not your love life." Peter was in his protective mother mode.

"I will. But this guy really piqued my interest. He's rich and educated, and so handsome." Then I added, "Hate saying goodbye. Drive carefully and stop worrying." Giving him a kiss on the cheek, "I love you so much."

I called Tony at the stroke of three the next day. We met for an early dinner at a small fish house in Marina del Rey specializing in tacos and wicked margaritas. Our first unofficial date. At least it was in my mind. We walked the harbor talking about boats and travel and family. I told my story calmly with no mistakes, and he told his. Youngest of four sons, his father lavished the boys with luxury. All were employed by the senior Safra's empire. Tony was in charge of Caribbean marketing but spent a great deal of time in California, mostly Silicon Valley, learning and obtaining the latest and greatest in communications software. At thirty-five, he had not yet married but said he was looking to settle down.

"It's time", he said. "This partying must stop. But the right woman is elusive, like a white dolphin or that big yeti foot."

I thought the comparison was rather strange but then asked, "And what would that woman be like, Tony?"

"Well, she would be self-assured, beautiful and definitely not a social climber. Did you email my father with some suggestions of art pieces?"

"Yes, but as we explained a more comprehensive inventory search is necessary. We'll have a better picture of what we can get in a few days."

I felt so relaxed with my new Latin friend. He didn't pry too deeply, which was a relief. I had insisted on driving myself to the harbor, mainly because I could never allow him to come to my humble apartment. If a relationship blossomed, this would eventually be a problem – one I had no idea how to solve. Our good night at my car wasn't overly romantic, leaving me envious of every woman he had kissed. Then I remembered, this was business, with just a dollop of a date. Okay, it was a little romantic.

I called Peter as soon as I got home and told him every detail, down to how while at the taco place, Antonio had brushed a wisp of hair from my eyes and let his hand rest on my face for a moment. "He took charge, Peter, and ordered a special margarita for me that he said was created in Brazil. Everything that came out of his mouth sounded so sexy. *Constance, you're an amazing woman. I want to see you again.*" Peter laughed at my attempt at a Portuguese accent.

"Then I answered, *Yes, a margarita sounds perfect.* Peter, later he put his hand on my cheek again and gently kissed me. My heart almost stopped."

"And . . .?" Peter wanted more. I could hear his curiosity through the phone.

"He opened my car door, gave me a little kiss and I drove off. But I replayed the goodbye and kiss over and over all the way home. Wonder I didn't have an accident.

And to top it off, I know he plans to buy several pieces of art. I'll be rolling in some serious commission."

Peter jumped in, "Again, I'm not sure mixing business and pleasure is a good idea, Connie. Better watch out. Do you want to see him again?"

"Silly question. Of course, we're going out on his dingy tomorrow night and he's bringing dinner."

"Oh Lord," Peter grumbled. "That's enough to make me barf. Dingy and dinner. Too bloody romantic for me."

I sensed Peter was getting a little jealous, so for the next ten minutes, our conversation was all about him and his hot romance.

"Peter, I've got to get some rest. More tomorrow. Hey, I just realized we're both seeing guys with the same name."

"Sweetie, I'm fucking my Tony. You're just flirting with yours. I win!"

CHAPTER TEN

Rothstein puffed away on his smelly cigar as he stood in the doorway of my office. "I got a call from Safra. Said he received the pictures and memo you emailed. God bless being tech savvy. Right? He's very interested in the small Miro as well as the water color Dali and both Peter Max paintings." Rothstein turned to leave, then, "Oh, he also liked the Alexandra Nikita. Good work, kid. Now, you have to close the deal. Almost three hundred thou on your first consult. Not bad."

Not bad? At six percent commission that would be eighteen thousand dollars, half of last year's total salary. Fantastic!

"Thank you. I have a meeting at the yacht tomorrow late afternoon. Hopefully, I'll be able to close over dinner."

Rothstein started to walk down the hall but again turned back and swaggered to my door. "Tomorrow night? Change it. Make it earlier. I need a plus one at a gallery opening on Rodeo at three and then a cocktail party at the Gabor mansion around seven. The Mrs. is at a spa."

Rothstein flicked ashes from his cigar into a plant on my desk and leaned in close to my face revealing his tobacco stained teeth and stank breath. "You know, Gabor's husband, the Prince, bought his title. Sad example of a man."

My stomach catapulted to my throat. I knew I had to say something immediately but my brain felt like it was on hold. I cleared my throat, "Oh, I wasn't aware. How could someone do that? So nice Mrs. Rothstein is having some spa time. I've never been to one. I mean in California." I blithered.

"There's a lotta quacks out there, Constance. Prince Von Gabor thinks he owns this town." Rothstein snapped his suspenders and left. I started to hiccup. Was he on to me, or was this pure coincidence? I had only worked at PC a few days and was pretty sure I hadn't slipped up. The perspiration on my palms and brow told a different story. Self-doubt swamped my thinking. I sat in my swivel chair and looked out to Wilshire Blvd. hoping the bustle of the city would be a distraction. It didn't work. I closed my office door, took off my shoes and did controlled breathing exercises for at least ten minutes. The chirping noises in my head stopped. I could breathe again.

My next task was to call Antonio's cell and change our

meeting. *Don't blow this deal.* Deep down, I was more interested in this gorgeous Brazilian than my commission. I had only met him twice but his charisma made my knees weak and heart race. A girl just knows when it's right.

"Antonio, Tony. Hi. Sadly, I have to change our appointment tomorrow. Business."

"That's too bad. My father must have really liked what you sent over. He texted that we would be getting some art. I was looking forward to our dingy ride."

"Me, too. I have a gallery opening and cocktail party. Can we make it earlier in the day? That way I can discuss some possible other choices and still be available to my boss."

"No. I'm afraid earlier won't work." Tony was quick and matter of fact. "Maybe my father will have some decisions by Thursday. Why don't you come over then, around seven? We'll have that, how you say, picnic and take a little boat ride."

"It's a date." I put down the phone. Ugh. Why did I say that? Why did I call it a date?

"Mary, want to grab lunch?" The morning had gone by quickly and I was famished.

"Sure, Lady C. I'll let the answering service know we'll

be out." Mary gathered her purse and sweater while I went to the rest room.

My lunch companion looked annoyed as I came back to the lobby. "Can't go, Constance." She waved me over to her desk. "Twibble wants to talk to you and the only time she has free today is now." She motioned for me to lean closer. "She's a witch with a capitol B. So, watch yourself. I think she's pissed that the newbie may have made a big sale."

Alone time with Juliet was not how I wanted to spend my lunch hour. I was craving potato pancakes. This would be our first one-on-one except for in- office pleasantries. I put my purse back in my desk drawer and waited. In about ten minutes, Juliet emerged shouting "Get your butt in here, Constance. We're eating in and your Top Ramen is getting cold."

CHAPTER ELEVEN

I had never met anyone quite like Juliet Twibble. To me, she looked sophisticated, attractive and self-assured. Tall, thin, dark haired and in her mid-thirties, this woman exuded confidence, power and brains.

But after our cup of soup lunch, my opinion changed.

Juliet tried to make small talk, even though she obviously cared less about how my day was going or the nice weather.

I knew from receptionist Mary that Juliet came from a very middle-class family. She professed her upbringing was privileged and I wasn't about to disclose her little secret. I thought to myself *this was an office of deceit*. Juliet continued. "I began my University career in Santa Clara. Small university there. Private." She smiled while adjusting the collar of her blouse. "My father came into a huge sum of money during my sophomore year and off I went to the Sorbonne."

"That must have been amazing," Connie interjected.

"It was." Juliet admitted. A half smile on her face. "I

was top of my class and as an American, I had to work twice as hard. An incredible experience and I've never looked back."

I nodded as Juliet stopped long enough to take a sip of coffee.

"Constance, I've been the number one selling consultant here for the past seven years. My career has skyrocketed. Just because you had some beginners luck, don't think you have a chance of unseating me. Rothstein may consider you his prize princess this week but I'm the reigning queen." The meanness in Twibble's voice came through loud and clear. Threatening, followed by a sickening sweetness. "Now tell me something I don't know about you."

I wanted to ask her why she was so angry and how her father came into so much dough but instead gave her the ten-minute version of my past, making sure I emphasized the snooty boarding schools and lineage to the real Queen. She didn't seem impressed. No reaction. It was all matter of fact. Only question she asked was, "Constance, did you have sheep on your estate in England?"

Weird! In the office she spoke like a sailor, pretended to be aristocratic to clients and asked bazaar questions.

I answered. "No, Juliet. We had cows."

The only other reference she made to my pending art deal was if it did close, she hoped I would spend my commission wisely. "Invest carefully, my dear. This business is as fickle as a bitch in heat."

"Thank you, Juliet, for the soup and fascinating chat. I had best get back to work. Heard Debbi Fields might be at the gallery opening later today and wants to expand her collection. You know Fields, the Cookie Queen."

"Say hi to Debs for me. Wish I could go. I'm meeting with a wealthy CEO from Atlanta. Huge potential client. Oh, and Constance, welcome. I'm thrilled you have joined us."

The gallery opening was amazing. A harpist played Bach fugues in the center of the room, engulfing the space with opulent music. Compositions for the sophisticated ear. Against the far back wall, a long table was filled with appetizers and dainty plates for self-serve. Waiters roamed filling crystal flutes with Dom Perignon while other white gloved servers carried silver trays piled high with tiny open sandwiches of egg salad, cucumbers, crème freche and caviar. The place was crowded with men and women dressed to impress. I gathered these were prospective buyers who carried platinum and black plastic to purchase expensive art.

Mr. Rothstein introduced me to everyone. "I'd like you to meet my new art consultant, Lady Constance Widford. She's new in town and absolutely brilliant." I was in heaven. These were the people I longed to be like. Their jewels were real and their Channel and Givenchy suits genuine. Men wore Gautier and Tom Ford with shoes that had to cost more than my entire wardrobe.

"Very pleased to meet you, Mrs. Fields. I love your cookies." Thank God I had overhead a man call her Debbie, and I put two and two together. "I so admire your ingenuity. You were the first."

"Thank you, Lady Constance. It's an honor to meet you. You must stop by my place and help me pick out some new pieces." At that moment, the cookie maven took my arm and walked me to a small oil by Gauguin. "What do you think, dear? Worth four hundred thousand?"

"Mrs. Fields, the value of art is in the eyes of the buyer. But any Gauguin is a great investment. I just love the warm colors, don't you? He painted it in Tahiti in 1894 or '95. That actually was his sail boat." I couldn't believe I was talking to the Cookie Queen suggesting that four hundred thousand was a steal. I was also ten inches away from an original Paul

Gauguin. Heaven. If nothing else, I knew my art.

"You're right, Constance, if I may I call you that. I want a Gauguin in my collection. Call me tomorrow and we'll discuss. Actually, come on by my house around three. I'm sure you can get me a deal. I'd rather go through you than the gallery." With that, she handed me her card and gave me a double cheeked kiss. The lips of someone who was royalty to me – and all Mall Shoppers in America – had touched my face. She knows my name. Yes, Lady Me was on a roll.

There he was in full formal, royal attire; epaulettes on his shoulders and a shiny satin sash. The Prince was holding court in the ballroom of his Bel Air estate. Sadly his wife, Zsa Zsa, was ill and couldn't attend the soiree.

As we approached his royal phoniness, Mr. Rothstein whispered, "You don't have to bow or curtsey. Nothing like that. He's just a down to earth Prince. Unzips his fly and pees like the rest of us."

Until minutes before entering this house, I thought our offices were the ugliest space I had ever seen. But this home took the cake as the crown jewel of over-the-top gaudiness. All four walls of the ballroom were covered in purple padded silk with at least three huge oil portraits of royal-looking people hanging by thick braided ropes. Then there were the paintings of the Prince and his dog, the Prince in a pasture and the Prince with a young Zsa Zsa. That one was actually very charming. The floor was large squares of black and white marble that looked like a chess board for giants. There was an antique concert grand Steinway in the center of the room and lots of men dressed like penguins serving food from trays.

I was mesmerized. *I'm in a room full of faux intelligentsia and possible real wealth.* What a day. I guessed most of these people were nouveau riche and wanted to pal around with others that might improve their status. But I didn't care. To me, this was the reason I became a Lady. I felt important. I felt empowered. I felt like I mattered. Then, I felt someone tapping my shoulder.

"Would you like some Champagne?" A bald man, wearing black horn-rimmed glasses, interrupted my minute of reverie. "I'm Stuart Evans, lawyer."

"Pleased to meet you, Mr. Evans. I'm Constance Widford."

"I know. Your reputation precedes you, My Lady. Quite a coup for good old Rothstein. A Noble amongst his stable." Evans let out a hardy laugh as he gave me a *good ol' boy* slap on the back, allowing his hand to linger a smidge too long. "Next thing he'll do is hire Tom Cruise to be his spokesperson." Now he was laughing uncontrollably. "By the way," wiping the tears from his eyes, " I handle all of Al's business dealings. Contracts, negotiations. I also date your colleague, Juliet Twibble."

I smiled but didn't say a word as the lawyer dabbed his nose with a cocktail napkin, caught his breath and continued.

"That Julia's smart, Constance. And I'm shrewd." He grinned and handed me a glass of bubbly from a waiter's tray. "You new in town?"

"Yes, Mr. Evans. I arrived a few weeks ago." *This man is strange.*

"Enjoying your work?" His tone was now serious.

"Very much, although I've just started."

"Watch yourself. This town shows no mercy. And Rothstein, he doesn't put up with shit."

I didn't know if I should thank the lawyer for his advice or argue that my boss seemed sweet. Before I could decide, the unattractive attorney bid me adieu. "Ciao, Constance. See you around the campus."

As I drank the delicious wine Evans had handed me, acutely cognizant of how I held the glass, I did an instant replay of our brief encounter. First impression was that he looked like a 1920's mobster with a twitchy eye and pitted complexion. I may have shrunk my stomach over the past few months, but my gut instincts were to be wary. What a pair, I thought. Twibble and Evans. I was no match for those two. They could eat me alive and spit me out like a bad piece of sushi. Hopefully, they will keep their distance and my wariness will have been for naught.

CHAPTER TWELVE

I kicked off my heels, shimmied out of my fake Prada suit and pulled on a ripped oversized Target tee that served as my nightshirt. It had been a long day but I really needed my nightly therapy chat with Peter.

"Hey, can you talk?" I flopped down on the couch, held the phone between my ear and shoulder and massaged my aching left foot.

"What's up, darlin'?"

"Am I interrupting something?" For a second, I swore I heard voices in the background.

"No. Just relaxing. Chomping on some chocolate covered raisins. Watching HBO. Talk on."

I was still on an adrenalin high from the gallery opening plus the soirée at the Prince's mansion. All had gone smoothly. Well, except my uncomfortable encounter with Rothstein's attorney. There was something ominous, scary about that man. And I don't mean just his looks.

"And then he said to me, I date Juliet Twibble. Like I care? Was he trying to intimidate me?"

"You're way too sensitive, Connie. He was probably just trying to set boundaries and let you know his place on the totem pole. What's up with the hunk from Brazil?"

"Had to cancel our appointment but will see him tomorrow." I noticed some spilled ketchup on the floor next to the refrigerator and wiped it up with a paper towel. "I'm getting all these signals that he's attracted to me, Peter, and I'm certainly to him. Is that possible after only two meetings?"

"Of course. Love, or at least lust at first sight. Funny you should call. I was about to ring you up with some big news. Really big news."

"What?"

"Are you ready?" Peter continued without giving me a chance to answer. "I'm thinking of proposing to my Tony. There, I said it."

I was silent.

"Hello, I just said I may get engaged. Anyone there?"

I pulled the phone away from my ear to protect it from the loud thumping emanating from the receiver. Peter was probably hitting the phone on the coffee table.

"Yes, I'm here. Just a lot to digest. Does he have any idea?" I tossed the dirty paper towel in the garbage, making a perfect basket from eight feet. "When do you think you'll do it?" My heart was pounding. Peter, engaged? Best Friend taken away from me by the Revlon relative.

I could hear that Peter was excited. He was squealing.

"I'm thinking of popping the question this Saturday. I'll cook a romantic dinner. After, maybe take him to Spa Casino. You know, we met for the first time in front of a Three Cherries slot machine two years ago. Friends, BALS, then lovers. Can you come down on Sunday to celebrate? Please, please?"

I walked to the frig and grabbed a light beer. "Of course. I'll be wherever you want."

Why wasn't I thrilled? As we talked, I paced in a circle around the couch and ripped off the tee shirt that now felt like it was strangling me.

"Peter, why don't you two live together? Partners. Why an official engagement?"

"OMG!" Peter dragged out the letters as he spoke. "Of all people I thought you would certainly understand. Can't believe you're questioning my choices. For your information, Lady, Tony moved in a few days ago. We are living together. Whatever. Later, Connie. I'm finished. Done. Just another example of how life has become all about you."

He slammed the phone down.

I was shocked.

He was right.

The drive down to the desert took about two hours. No freeway traffic at ten P.M. Plenty of time to plan my apology. I had become obsessed with my transformation and journey. After all he had done for me, I needed and wanted to be there for Best Friend and his joy.

Peter opened his front door wearing only pajama bottoms. He obviously had been sleeping and was shocked to see me. "What the . . . ?"

I hugged the tall galoot and started to cry. "I'm so sorry. I love you. You're my best friend. I'd never . . . "

We talked it through over a glass of merlot, maybe two. Tony was fast asleep in the bedroom. He never came out. This was between Peter and me.

"I need some fresh air. Emotional overload!" Peter was almost hyperventilating as he threw on jeans and a sweater and bolted out the front door. "Come on," he insisted. "You've had enough to drink."

We headed for the twenty-four-hour Wal Mart in Rancho Mirage and walked around the huge box store, arm in arm, swigging a bottle of Starbuck's Frappuccino grabbed from aisle fifty-seven. Between Dog Food and Electronics, I expressed my happiness for him and how sorry I was for not recognizing the deep love he had for his handsome lover.

An hour later, I was on the freeway driving back to my faux castle in my make-believe world.

There's something soothing, almost hypnotic, about driving on an empty California freeway in the middle of the night. The glow of exit signs blends with oncoming headlights. It's quiet. No horns, no sirens. The only noise on the drive home was in my head.

My reaction to Best Friend's exciting news threw me. Was I afraid of losing Peter or was it something much darker? Every day for the past several weeks I'd woken mostly with excitement and positive anticipation of what the day would bring. I had accomplished physically and emotionally more in the past six months than I had in the past six years. I was experimenting, learning and questioning.

But there was also the gnawing fear of being discovered. The "what ifs" were part of my daily thoughts and the task of pushing them down was daunting.

And the burning question - was my new life making me happy? The expectation of becoming Lady Constance had been monumental. The work to get to the finish line was arduous but exhilarating. The end product, so far, was everything I had dreamt it would be.

"A mocha latte, no whip, Vente, two Splendas, nonfat." I had pulled off the freeway and drove through a twenty-four-hour Starbucks. I needed more caffeine. The cool night air also helped.

Back on the road, I thought about how in the past week I had met scions of industry, artists of acclaim and a rich, handsome billionaire's son. So why doubt what I had created?

As I drove into my parking garage, I spoke out loud. It was almost a mantra. Lady Widford, relax. You are who you think you are. Your journey has just begun. Let no one tell you otherwise.

The bullshit sounded good.

CHAPTER THIRTEEN

The motor boat skipped past the breakers and plowed through waves like a bullet aiming for its target. The sun was warm, the salty spray sticky, making it difficult to see through my fake Gucci sunglasses. Antonio stood at the helm and steered with perfection as I held on for dear life.

"Freedom. That's what speed and salt water in your face is about." He yelled to be heard over the scream of the seventy-five horses driving the eighteen-foot dingy. "Wahoo. This is fantastico." His Brazilian accent made the simplest words sound sexy. *Fantastico*. Much more seductive than plain *Fantastic*. Antonio smiled at me. "Want to take the wheel?"

"Not if you value your life. I've never driven a boat."

"Look around, my dear." Antonio bent towards me and was speaking inches from my ear. His hot breath sent shivers through my body. "There's nothing to worry about. Only water and sky," he paused inching closer, "and your beautiful face."

Wow. My heart seemed to be doing the samba. A bead of perspiration found its way slowly down my neck, between my breasts, trapped by the underwire of my bra.

I looked at him…this Latin Adonis at the helm, the wind blowing his black hair straight back, tight cotton tee pressed against his chest. My breath caught. This god of a man bestowed me with a compliment. Life is complete.

"Yes, show me what to do." I would have piloted a jet or fought a Ninja if he had asked.

I grabbed Antonio's outstretched arm and took his hand, maneuvering my clumsy body carefully in front of his. There I was, firmly holding onto the steering wheel for dear life as Latin God wrapped his arms around me, pressing his body close. I smelled the scent of his woodsy cologne. All man, his strong hands wrapped around my waist. His body heat countered the cold from the blasting wind.

"You were meant to be at sea, Constance." He pushed his knees into the back of mine. "That's right. Bend a little. Just ride the rhythm of the ocean. Loose knees, relax. Up and down. Up and down."

Oh, good God, I felt warm in places that had been cold most of my life.

Antonio's hands moved from my waist to the wheel,

intertwining his fingers with mine. His body pushed even closer.

"Turn around," he whispered. "I have the wheel."

I obeyed. The wind now against my back, I looked into my client's eyes. He kissed me - soft, nice.

Suddenly, the craft jolted to a stop. Antonio had switched off the power. He kissed me again. This time with more passion.

"Lady Constance, I want to – how you say, make beautiful love to you." I stared at Antonio in shock.

The mood had turned from movie scene romantic to scary slasher headlines . . . *British Nobility Found Washed Up on Marina del Rey Beach. Investigation Uncovers She Was A Fraud but owned the land.* I was out on the ocean with a man I barely knew, who owned half of Brazil and who apparently liked to make love on a pint-sized boat in public.

"What?" I finally found my voice. "I'm flattered, Tony. I am. And lord knows it's tempting." I cleared my throat. Oh, if he only knew how enticing his offer was. "But you are my client and I momentarily lost track of that. Anyway, this is hardly the time or place. Sorry if I mislead you. Let's go back. Now." I was stern. Professional. Part of me wanted to strip down to my Victoria Secrets and ravish every inch of Latin God. But the conservative, button downed Victorian in me prevailed.

"As you wish, My Lady. Know that taking you right here would have been my utmost pleasure and hopefully yours." Then out of nowhere, he said. "I'm hungry. I need food. To shore we go."

Antonio started the engine and we zipped back to the marina not saying one word to each other. Dinner was meatball sandwiches and beer at an Italian deli close to his dock. We ate on a park bench.

I questioned if I was being a prude. The only accountability I had was to

myself. Connie Botello would never have sex in public. Morals too strict and

self-esteem too low.

Lady Constance, well, she's still a virgin.

CHAPTER FOURTEEN

"You have an admirer." Mary yelled as I whisked past her desk on the way to my office.

"You're fifteen minutes late." Rothstein was playing catch in the hall with his ever present four-legged companion.

"Sorry. Traffic." Duke lumbered over and planted a wet kiss on my cheek when I bent over to pet him.

On my desk a single red rose stood tall in a clear glass container with a hand written note: *Voce e o por do sol. You are the sunset* (with a line through it and the word *sunshine* put in) *of my life.*

"Mary, who delivered the flower?" I returned to the lobby. The message had been written on a pad from The Hilton.

"It was a very good-looking man, about thirty or so, tan, black hair and wearing a red tee shirt and white slacks. Yummy, honey."

"Brazilian accent?" I asked. Mary nodded and gave me

a lascivious grin.

It had to have been Antonio. Why a single rose? He could afford five dozen. Why deliver it himself?

Back in my office, I got on my cell. "From a man's point of view, what does it mean?" I asked Best Friend.

"Okay, first, thanks for the man compliment. I'm feeling way macho these days. Did I tell you Tony and I went to . . . ."

"Back to me, Peter." I brushed the petals across my cheek. So soft. Reminded me of the kiss.

"Sorry, Connie. When only a single rose is sent it could mean that he's holding back. What color?"

"Red, long stem. In a clear vase."

"Oh sweetie, he's either as cheap as my grandpa Clive or has no clue how to woo a woman. You said he kissed you? How was that?"

"First, gentle. Then determined, forceful . . . rather wet. Made my toes curl. Am I reading too much into this? A dozen long stems would have been a better move. Right?" I walked to the back of my desk and plopped into my swivel chair. The side to side motion soothed me.

"Yes, a much better move, Sweetie. But don't write him off. Maybe the super wealthy play it cool and understated.

Gotta run. Customer. Ciao."

Mrs. Fields didn't buy the Gauguin. At least I got to meet the Cookie Queen. The senior Safra bought the Miro I had suggested, a Nikita and Peter Max for a total of two hundred-ninety-five thousand, making my commission around eighteen.

Amazing.

Safra's instructions were to deliver the art in about a month since the yacht was still undergoing construction and he didn't want his new possessions exposed to the dust. He also requested that I supervise the installation.

Over the next few weeks, I met with at least four potential clients. No other sales, but I was meeting fascinating people. They all zeroed in on my title, asked questions and invited me to parties …I assume to show me off to their friends. The rest of my time was spent doing research for pieces I could broker at bargain prices.

I lunched with Mary once a week and with Mr. Rothstein twice. Rothstein Junior had left on a buying trip to Italy, and Twibble was busy working with two Russian auto dealers reportedly worth billions.

"So, Constance, you've been here a little over three

weeks." Rothstein was chewing on a lamb shank as he spoke. We were lunching at Tahin on Westwood Blvd. near Wilshire, an upscale Jewish Persian area of Beverly Hills.

The restaurant was filled with Middle-eastern looking men and a few fashionably dressed women carrying Prada, Gucci or Hermes. And, of course, Duke was lying at Mr. Rothstein's feet waiting for a nibble. I ordered swarma and bastimi rice with bread the cook baked in an earthen oven smack in the middle of the dining area. The smell of grilled meat and hot spices made my mouth water. Nothing like this in Palm Springs. I vowed to just have no calorie lettuce for dinner.

Rothstein continued, "And what are your initial thoughts of the company?"

"I'm very happy, Mr. Rothstein." I dabbed around my mouth with the cloth napkin. "The meetings you've taken me to, the people I've met, well, they are amazing."

"I would have thought this level of socialization would be second nature to you." Rothstein let out a muffled belch.

Shifting in my seat, I mentally called for one of my rehearsed speeches.

"It's different. I was very sheltered growing up and didn't think our family was any better or worse off than my

Nanny's or Ernesto's, our gardener." And the fabrications continued. "When I left for University, I was surrounded by likeminded students with similar lineage and wealth. The people I've met through you are different. Most have become wealthy through their own ingenuity. I admire that."

I dipped my nan in the tahini sauce and waited for Rothstein to speak. When he didn't, I continued.

"Mr. Rothstein, what do you know about Mr. Safra? I've gone out with his son several times. Actually, I have a date with him tonight."

Rothstein put down his third lamb shank and took a gulp of his iced tea. "He's never mentioned a son. Do you want me to check him out?"

I couldn't answer Mr. Rothstein since my mouth was full of grilled lamb and tomatoes.

Rothstein continued after another loud sound emanated from his body. "I know Safra is legit. His son? I know nothing"

"Don't say anything." My voice was too animated. Last thing on earth I wanted was for my boss to be butting into my personal life. I should have never mentioned anything to him. Calming myself, I continued. "I have only seen Antonio three times. Was just wondering. Please don't bother his father. In fact, I would appreciate it if you didn't mention it at all. Let's keep everything professional."

"Done. Let's get back to the office. Although Constance, a relationship with a billionaire's son could be very intriguing."

I sat in the front seat of Mr. Rothstein's new Mercedes 550 L as he drove around the corner to my parked car. No valet service for me.

"Here you go." Rothstein said as I exited the car. "I'm meeting a possible new client at the tennis club at three and then Happy Hour with Twibble to catch up. Drive carefully."

I inhaled one last breath of 'new car smell' as I slammed the heavy door and unlocked my leased BMW. "Mr. Rothstein, thank you." I yelled through the front windows the valet had lowered.

"For what? You're our shining star."

"For lunch. For the opportunity. For understanding much more than you say."

"Shalom, Constance. I hate mush."

Their shining star. Ha! I was sure trying.

I should have asked Mr. Rothstein why Twibble's boyfriend, the lawyer, had been nosing around the office several days ago asking questions. Mary thought it had something to do with accounting.

Before leaving for Europe, the younger Rothstein asked for my London address. He wanted to look up my relatives. "Tea or dinner?" he inquired. I said they were on holiday in Spain. Next time.

Excuses, deceit and a gorgeous gazillionaire who wanted me.

This was the new life of Mr. Rothstein's star.

CHAPTER FIFTEEN

I'm not happy. The words were deafening, even though they were only in my mind. Even though I had just thanked Rothstein for all his company had done for me, something was missing. Six months ago, Lady Constance Whidford wasn't even a figment of my imagination. Then, with the click of a mouse, and months of hard work, I was her in body but not soul.

As I turned right off of Westwood Boulevard onto Wilshire, I ran my tongue over my teeth. The taste of tahini and lamb lingered. Bitter.

Happiness. Is it tied up in finding a man and having four kids? Or is it proving to others that you are worthwhile? Do others even care about your background? Is happiness realized by having simple goals or is it fulfilling big dreams; or in my case, living an extreme fantasy? My thoughts got darker.

On the picture board in my apartment I had taped magazine photos of Polo ponies being ridden on perfectly manicured green fields. Versace ads. Front and center were a brochure of diamond jewels from Harry Winston and a picture of my dream husband wearing white rolled up cotton slacks and a pale blue flowing dress shirt, the clothes he would wear on our beach walks when we vacationed in Antigua. Dreams on a white board in my rented efficiency.

Peter is happy – he's with Tony.

Twibble seems happy – she has her lawyer friend and a successful job.

Duke is happy. He has Wolfgang's scraps and Mr. Rothstein's lap.

All I've ever wanted was to be seen and loved.

The light turned red at Beverly Glen. I texted Peter. *Really need to see you. Tonight? I'll drive down? Not sure this Lady thing is working out. I'm suddenly questioning everything. It just may be too much. In a funk.*

The light turned green. I looked down at my phone. A response from Peter: *Can't tonight, Sweetie. Mom's having Tony and me over for dinner. Tomorrow?*

I typed back. *Can we talk? I'm really depressed. Questioning everythi…*

The last thing I recalled was driving by the massive entrance to The Wilshire Country Club and thinking maybe I'd like to have dinner there. Then noise. Loud, ear splitting, clanking noise.

I don't remember being taken out of the car or being put into the ambulance. I came to with sirens blaring and the face of a huge man hovering over me. His voice was soft and comforting.

"You are one lucky lady. Didn't your Mama tell you not to text and drive?" He had a Southern twang.

I tried to answer but the pain was excruciating. Every breath felt like a knife twisting inside my chest. Big EMT held a bandage on the left side of my head, pressing hard to stop the bleeding. The strong smell of disinfectant made me nauseous. I threw up.

"I'm so sorry." I was more embarrassed than sorry. "Am I going to die?" It hurt to talk. I was scared.

"The doctors will check you out. We're almost at Cedars Sinai. But between you and me," he whispered. "you'll be okay. Maybe a concussion because of the throwing up. Your head may need a few stitches. The light post on the other hand, well, the city and your insurance company will go around on that one, honey. You have medical?"

"Yes." Thank goodness Rothstein had covered me from day one.

"Follow my finger."

I obeyed the young doctor. She couldn't have been any older than thirty-five and Sports Illustrated beautiful. All business. Why didn't she smile? Her life was probably perfect. She had this Grey's Anatomy glamorous job and I'm sure all the young and old doctors in the ER were lusting after her. Maybe she had cellulite all over her ass.

Model perfect Doctor multitasked, continuing to speak while typing her report on a gadget that looked like a computer hanging from the wall. "No signs of severe head trauma but we'll get an MRI to make sure there's no internal bleeding. And I'll have my Intern wrap you. X-rays showed two cracked ribs. Anyone I should call? Husband? Parents?"

Why didn't she just pour alcohol on my open wounds? "I'm single and parents are deceased."

My answer stopped the doctor. "We'll be keeping you overnight for observation." A pause. "Here's your purse." She grabbed it from under the stretcher. "I won't look if you want to use your phone to call a friend. Not allowed but what the hell."

She was almost through the curtain of the examining room when she turned back, "I know who you are, Lady Constance. Newspapers. You did a stupid thing."

She knows who I am? How unfortunate that I have no clue.

I opened my eyes to see Peter looming over my bed. This was getting to be monotonous and a vision that I did not want repeated.

"I got here as soon as I could. You okay?" He kissed my forehead.

"Peter, how did you . . . ?"

"I was the last text on your phone. The police called. I freaked."

"I'll be alright. MRI was fine. Just hurts to talk. Cracked ribs." I started a small laugh as I held a pillow to my chest.

"What so funny?" Peter stroked my hair.

"Seems like we've done this hospital thing a little too much."

Best Friend smiled and held my hand while bringing me up to date on all the desert dirt. As usual, Peter was taking care of me and I felt calm, secure.

"Constance, oh my God. I came as soon as I heard. Baby, you Okay?" It was nine in the evening and Antonio rushed in carrying a bouquet of sunflowers.

I was shocked to see my – what was he – my boyfriend? My friend? The lover I had not slept with but had dabbled in some pretty heavy pre coitus kissing. "Antonio Safra, this is my best friend, Peter." The two eyed each other and finally shook hands.

"Antonio, how did you find out?" I held the pillow tight trying to lessen the pain.

Moving closer to the bed and elbowing Peter out of the way, Antonio spoke while kissing my hand and cheek. "My dear Constance. We had dinner plans tonight. Remember? We were picnicking on the beach in Santa Monica. Yes?"

My eyes went to the ceiling as if to say, of course, how could I have forgotten.

"So, when you didn't show up, I put an emergency call in to your office. Of course, the switch board connected me to a Miss Mary who found out what happened a half hour ago through your On Star service who called your business number. I rushed right here. Mr. Rothstein and Miss Mary are on their way. And a Twibble."

I was on drugs, mega pain killing barbiturates. "Antonio, would you give me a moment alone with Peter? I need him to help me with something. Just for a minute."

"My precious, Constance, I will help you with whatever you need. You are my, how you say, the lady of my sleep?"

I cleared my throat. "Dreams, Antonio?" His English

was selectively spotty.

"Si, my Constance. Si, dreams. I'll be just outside."

Antonio left, confused and probably hurt.

Peter closed the door and sat down on my bed.

"What is it? Talk."

"I'm not sure. I'm tired, groggy. I'm scared it's all unraveling." I hadn't cried since the accident, and now, the tear gates opened and poured down my cheeks.

Peter held me tight, telling me it would all work out. "Was it something in particular?"

"Yes." I squirmed and wiped my eyes. "Nix the hold, Peter. Too tight. Hurting." I had to speak softly and slowly, limiting my lungs from pushing on my immensely sore ribs. "Stuart Evans, Rothsteins lawyer, Twibble's boyfriend. I'm scared of him. He was so strange at the Gabor mansion, demeaning, almost threatening. If he insists I notify relatives or if there's an insurance problem, I'm afraid something will come up. Oh God, I could go to jail. I put my name as Constance Widford."

"We'll deal with that later. Do you remember the text you sent me saying how depressed you were?"

"Yes, kind of. I've been depressed for the last few days. Peter, is there a fine line between happiness and insanity? I feel both. I love what I'm doing, I really do. But something inside of me says run. What I'm doing is sort of wrong." The pain meds were really kicking in. "I'm legitimate, Peter. I own the land in England. I have the letters from the barrister."

"Yes, you're the real deal, Lady Constance. But remember, if Connie Botello ever wants to come home, she can. Now, close your eyes and go to sleep. I'll herd the troops away. Sounds like they're congregating outside."

"Don't leave me, Peter." I held onto his hand tightly.

"I'll be here all night."

"Did I tell you I've been invited to a party at the Scottish Ambassador's house this Friday?" I started to sing, "Whose looking under, the kilt of wonder?" Peter nodded as he stroked my head. I continued to babble. "Had tea with Jane Fonda last week and she asked me to find her a Lichten...Lichten...you know, that painter guy?" Peter nodded. "I think he likes me just for my title, Peter. So sad. But I don't care. He's so yummy and rich. No title, he would walk right on by." I started to sing again. "Walk on By. Walk on by." The pain killers were making me loopy.

I closed my eyes and heard Peter leave for the hallway and explain to Rothstein, Twibble, Mary and Antonio that I was sleeping.

"Does she need a private nurse?" Rothstein tried to whisper but his voice came through the closed door loud and clear.

Peter assured him I didn't. "See you all tomorrow. Not sure if she'll be released or kept another day. I'll tell Constance you were here."

Peter continued. "Antonio, please stay a minute." Amazing how strong and straight Best Friend's voice sounded.

"I know you're rich and obviously handsome." Peter cleared his throat before continuing. "But you do anything to hurt her and my team will come after you like a rat on cheese."

Couldn't believe that was my Peter speaking.

I could hear Antonio break into laughter. "You have a team?"

"Yes." Peter got louder. "And they can be ruthless. Tony, Steve, Bruce, if you must know. So, be careful Amigo. Be very, very careful."

Best Friend was protecting me. I finally could relax and sleep.

CHAPTER SIXTEEN

My time at home recuperating went quickly. No car, but delivery from local markets kept me in cottage cheese, yogurt, mashed potatoes and ice cream. Soft, comfort foods. After making sure I was okay, Peter went back to the desert. Offers from the office to come by with chicken soup were politely rejected.

"Mary, I know everyone means well, but I really just need rest. Catching up on some reading and Netflix series." I couldn't have a soul come over and see how I lived. My studio was nice but not befitting nobility.

My deep dark secret. I had used hair guru Bruce's cousin's Beverly Hills address on my W-2 and hadn't changed it since starting to work. They all thought I had a fancy address in a prime area. I was in so deep.

Antonio was the peskiest, calling at least three times a day. He certainly meant well and it was flattering, but there just wasn't much to talk about. Finally, three weeks after the accident, I said I'd meet him in Santa Monica in front of the waterfall on the Third Street Promenade. I now had a rental car provided by my insurance and was feeling much better.

The Promenade is a bustling shopping/eating area closed off to traffic and always packed with sightseers. Every block has two or three street entertainers – the reggae band, the classical violinist, the folk singer playing her guitar, the dog doing back flips. The smells of American and ethnic cuisine spilled from the restaurants, and storefronts tantalized with everything from surfer shorts to risqué sleepwear.

"You look rested. You feel good?"

"Yes, Tony, I feel great. Almost all better. A little sore. Back to work first thing tomorrow." It was good to see my client-friend-boyfriend.

"Wonderful. Hungry? How about El Gaucho?" Suddenly Antonio stopped and looked in my eyes. "Voce e tao linda, Constance."

Then the moment was over. He continued. "You like South American food? Si?"

El Gaucho was two blocks away.

White table clothes, rustic open beamed ceiling, dark oak walls and live pan flute music set the tone. Antonio talked me through the Argentinean menu, describing the cuisine with lip smacking gusto. Oh, those lips. I wanted them pressed to mine. Again, he was in a tight tee, yellow this time, and white slacks. By now, I recognized his dress as a uniform, his trademark and a way of showing off his incredible body.

"My treat tonight, Tony. After all, your Dad is buying some substantial art which gives me a very nice commission."

Latin God accepted.

One glass of dry red wine relaxed me. The crispy bread dipped in olive oil and herbed balsamic vinegar was heaven.

"Constance, tell me more." Antonio reached over and held my hand. "How, I mean, where have you lived? Your familia? Sister? Brother?"

"Waiter, another glass of wine, please." Why was I nervous? Was it his movie star looks? Or was it my insecurity dating a man with such wealth?

"After dinner, we go back to your place? Si? I'd take you to the yacht but with all the construction, not comfortable."

Oh Lord, how am I going to get out of this one?

"Funny you mention construction, Antonio. My place is being painted. The fumes are horrible. They just started today. I'm actually staying with a girlfriend for a few days." And the lies kept coming.

Antonio took my hand again and kissed my palm. "I want to be with you, Constance. How can we arrange this?"

I squirmed before answering. Not sure if it was the wine or the raw aching to have sex that gave me the courage to answer. "There's a little hotel down the street. It's right on the ocean, Shutters. Pricey but beautiful. Why don't you see if they have a room?"

"My English and understanding is so bad, Constance. You make reservation. My Dad will reimburse. You know, a consultation." Antonio looked at me with his smoldering eyes and I was gone.

It had been four years since I had sex. Last time was with a guy named Jim who picked me up at The Daily Grill in Palm Desert. I was at the counter, waiting for my "to go" order. He was having a Happy Hour Gin and Tonic. We talked about baseball and then...? The sex was horrible. He was out of my apartment in thirty minutes and never called. Peter gave me hell for being so available. I gave myself props for at least insisting on a condom.

"We have a room. They'll hold it until 10 PM."

The rest of dinner was like a sexy tango. Each bite of steak, each lick of the hot chimichurri sauce brought us closer to dessert.

Shutters is like a New England hotel with a pinch of California chic and a dab of hobo pizzazz. It's not pretentious, more comfortable. I signed at the front desk for the room - $796, ocean view, feeling a bit like a call girl. It was strange Antonio didn't carry a credit card. Was my desire to be loved overshadowing logic?

The small balcony looked straight out onto the Pacific. Too bad it was nine thirty at night. Couldn't see a thing. Stalling, I pretended to be engrossed with the smell of the salt water and sound of the waves.

Antonio, meanwhile, took a quick shower and emerged wearing only a towel snuggly wrapped around his thirty-two-inch waist. Seeing him stand in the brightly lit hotel room sent tingles to all the right places. He was beautiful. And he wanted me. He wanted Connie Botello, Italian orphan whose best friends were gay, who'd had never traveled further than San Diego and who six months ago weighed forty pounds more.

No! He doesn't want me. He wants Lady Constance. The woman he wants to make love to is wealthy and a noble, a woman he would be proud to bring home to billionaire daddy.

Screw the mental conflict. I AM Lady Constance. I

OWN the land in England and I legally and spiritually have embodied the person he thinks I am.

Antonio joined me on the balcony.

"Beautiful Constance." He kissed my neck and I shuddered from the softness of his lips against my skin.

"Come, my dear. To bed."

With no resistance, Antonio led me inside to what I was sure would be paradise.

"Leave the balcony doors open. I love the sound." While Latin God made sure my wish was granted, I searched for light switches. No lights. Maybe one in the bathroom.

"Leave the lights on. I want to devour your beauty." Antonio's voice was almost demanding.

"No, I'm freer with the lights off. Please." Antonio reluctantly agreed.

With the sound of waves lapping against the sand and Antonio's body lapping against mine, we made mediocre love. I expected more. I thought I would be transported to a new world. Bells would toll the arrival of that magical moment when I climaxed into Latin God's arms screaming the deity's name. Instead, I faked it as the weight of his sweaty body crushed mine.

"That was amazing, Constance. You're a great lover."

Antonio rolled over leaving me exposed, vulnerable and horny. "What time is it?"

"It's ten thirty." I answered.

"Oh lord, I need to get back to the yacht. Expecting phone calls from Europe in an hour."

With that, Latin God dressed and thanked me profusely for a perfect evening.

"You're amazing, Lady Constance. And you're my special sweet. Are you staying the night?"

"Might as well. They don't rent these rooms by the hour. How will you get back to the boat?"

"I called an Uber when I was in the bathroom. It will be here in five minutes. Ciao, bella Constance."

With a kiss on the forehead and a slap on my butt, Antonio was gone.

CHAPTER SEVENTEEN

F og horns woke me at five in the morning. After a quick shower, I dressed and checked out via the television app.

The ten dollars I forked over for a dry bagel at the lobby breakfast stand made me wince, but I was hungry. Then there was the thirty-five-dollar valet. I felt like crap and looked even worse with wet hair and no makeup. I had the *Morning After Sex Regrets*.

By nine I had transformed myself into a respectable art consultant and was ready to take on whatever challenges Mr. Rothstein had for the day. But Rothstein had the flu and young Rothstein was meeting clients in San Francisco. My first day back would be spent with Mary and Juliet Twibble.

"How's the Argentinean?" Twibble had a cheese Danish in one hand and a huge mug of coffee in the other.

I answered as nonchalantly as I could. "He's Brazilian. We had dinner. Does the bump on my forehead look horrible?" I wanted to divert her questioning.

"Are you going to see him again?" But the questions

kept coming.

"I don't know. I guess so. I'll only be working a few hours today. Doctor recheck at 2 PM." I really didn't have an appointment.

"Constance, when you have a minute, I'd like to see you in my office. We need to talk." Twibble's voice was cold. Hearing this from a boyfriend, those words mean "it's over." Coming from a co-worker . . . ?

What did she want? *Relax. Breath. Blink.* Maybe it was just a new assignment. I cleared my throat.

"I'm free now, Juliet." My voice cracked like a thirteen-year-old boy. "Mary, please hold my calls." I really wasn't expecting any but it sounded like the thing to say.

Juliet Twibble. I was so uncomfortable with this woman. She sat behind her pristine desk, took out a mirror from her top drawer and checked her teeth for bits of breakfast. When sure her mouth hygiene was impeccable, the ice witch took out a manila file and slammed it on the desk. Not sure if she saw my body jump.

"Explain this." Her voice was low but forceful.

I had no idea what she was talking about and drew further back in my seat like it were my protective cocoon.

"Constance, we sent flowers three weeks ago to the

address you gave us. According to the florist, you don't reside on Clarkson Drive in Beverly Hills and never have. You lied on your insurance form?"

"No. I didn't. That's where I was living when I first got to Los Angeles. No lies." I was lying.

Twibble continued. "You know Stuart, right? My boyfriend. Our attorney?"

I nodded.

"Well, a few days ago he did a background check. Something we should have done before you ever started working here. We naively believed Mr. Rothstein's friend." Twibble got up and leaned across the desk. "My dear, lovely Lady, we found the web site where you bought the title. You are a fake, as fake as that Chanel you're carrying and the diamond earrings you're wearing. Fake, fake and fake."

Those words. She drew them out and punctuated each with such orgasmic pleasure that I thought she was going to explode. Again, the venomous words expounded. "You are a Fake with a capital F." A wry smile came over her face, like a cat who had just caught a mouse and was ready to devour it.

I didn't move. I didn't talk.

"Well, aren't you going to defend yourself?" Juliet's

nostrils flared.

After taking a deep cleansing breath, I stood and looked directly at the witch. "I have nothing to defend. I am Lady Constance Widford. I own land outside of London. I am a noble and I have a Master's degree in art history."

"Yes, you may have an online degree but you don't have a title. You're trailer trash. A social climber of the worse kind. My Lady, Mr. Rothstein has given me the authority to let you go. Mary has your final paycheck. No severance. You, despicable liar, "Twibble inhaled. "are… " She spit out the words from her gut. "royally fired."

CHAPTER EIGHTEEN

It happened so fast. I was blindsided.

Mary handed me a brown bag and I filled it with the few personal items I had stored in my office. The Plain Jane receptionist was shocked. "I'm so sorry, Constance. It's not true, right?"

"Of course, it's not true, Mary. Well, most of it isn't. For some reason Twibble wants me gone. I'll prove to her and that lawyer bottom feeder boyfriend of hers and Mr. Rothstein that I am Lady Constance Widford. This is ridiculous. I know who I am."

But again, I didn't. I walked to the parking garage with tears running down my cheeks and a heart so heavy I thought it would burst all over Canon Drive. Everything was a blur. I had put the envelop Mary handed me in my purse and held tightly on to the grocery bag as if it stored treasures. Maybe I thought it did. All the mementoes of Lady Constance were stuffed in a paper bag, tattered and weak from use and mishandling, like me. I was blaming others for the shattered world I had created myself.

***

The back door to California Desert Art was unlocked. The familiar smell of the stock room momentarily comforted me as I walked through to the main gallery. I stood motionless looking like one of the famous colored ceramic statues standing majestically against the side wall. But I wasn't famous and I certainly didn't feel majestic. I felt like Connie Botello and not Lady Widford.

"I am Lady Widford." The words came blaring out of my mouth like an exploding pressure cooker. Best Friend was helping an older woman. Two other tourist type men wearing Bermuda shorts and Izod polos were looking at a piece of glass art by a local artist. All stopped in midsentence, caught their breath and stared at what they surely must have thought was a crazed lady ready to rob the gallery and steal their wallets.

"Connie?" Peter looked at me, then his clients, back at me and continued. "If you all would excuse me for a minute, I need to attend to something – ah, someone." He crossed the length of the store, took my arm and escorted me back to the storage room.

"Connie, what is going on? Have you fucking lost your

mind?"

I just kept shaking my head up and down and side to side. "They found out. They said I'm not Lady Constance and that I'm a fraud. And then they fired me. That's it. That's all. My life is ruined. Kill me now."

Peter sat me down in a chair behind my old desk, opened the small refrigerator under the sink in the kitchen area, handed me a bottle of Skinny Girl Margarita and a paper cup. "Stop being so dramatic. Drink. I'll close down as soon as I finish with these customers." He kept talking as he walked away. "And don't kill yourself. That would be bad PR for the gallery."

Peter's condo felt different now that Tony had moved in. It was homier. More floral arrangements and fewer nude pictures of men. I continued my drinking, moving on to peach flavored vodka on the rocks.

"Here's a pajama top to sleep in and a new tooth brush. Sheets in the guest room are clean. Tony is bringing home some Chinese for dinner. Think you can eat?" Peter was being his endearing self.

"Not hungry. Can I have a sheet of paper and pen? I need to start a list."

Peter handed me a pad and pencil and sat on the couch.

"What? What are you staring at?" I asked the lumbering giant. "It's my reality. I need to start canceling things. Can I stay here a few days?" Best Friend didn't answer. He just continued to smile and watch as I started to write.

"Number one: give notice to landlord. Two: Cancel utilities. Three: Oh my God, I need to call Antonio. If he doesn't hear from me, he'll go to the office and they'll tell him why I was fired."

Peter rubbed my arm. "Sweetie, you need to tell him."

"No." I said emphatically, pulling away. "I'll text him and just say I was called away on business for a couple of weeks. Europe. Maybe France or England."

I looked at Peter and slowly got up and rounded the coffee table. "You know what, Peter? I WILL go to England. I have a document signed by a barrister. I legally own that land outside of London. I'll go to his office, get another document certifying my title and bring it back to Rothstein. I'll take pictures. Barristers can't lie. They take an oath or something. It would be fraud if they did."

I was manic and pacing.

"Rothstein will see the papers and the pictures and beg me to come back. Peter, give me your lap top. I need to find a flight. Do you know a hotel in London? How do I get from

Heathrow into the city?"

Peter watched; his mouth slightly open. Eventually, he got up, stopped me mid step and wrapped me in his arms. "You are not going to London. You will close up your Los Angeles place and come back to work here."

"NO!" I screamed breaking away. "I am going to London. I need to prove to myself and all those Rothsteins that my title is legitimate." I quieted myself and continued. "I need to do this, Peter. I need to go and be face to face with the man who made me a Lady."

"Connie," Peter's voice was low and sincere. "You made yourself a Lady."

126

CHAPTER NINETEEN

Three days later I was on American Flight 136 from Los Angeles to Heathrow. Antonio seemed to accept my sudden business trip. I promised to keep in touch. Peter thought I was certifiably insane but the need to prove my believed truth was stronger than any logic. The check I had received on my last day of work was for $18,735. – commission from the several pieces of art Antonio's father had purchased. This nest egg would take me to London, house me in a modest hotel for a few days while I met with the Barrister from Elite Titles. I made a binder of what the company had sent me, the address of the purchased land, all of their Internet information, my credit card receipt and email correspondence. I was armed and ready for my mission.

"Yes, thank you." I accepted a glass of red wine from the flight attendant and added, "I'd like the fettuccini, please. Or is the salmon better?"

The older woman answered that I should definitely take the pasta.

Nine in the evening. If after dinner I watched a movie, slept for six hours, had breakfast and read a few magazines, the flight would almost be over. I was scheduled to land at two twenty in the afternoon, would take a train or Underground to London, have dinner, shower, sleep and be ready to get answers in the morning. Thank God for the Internet. I was prepared.

This was my first time out of the country. I had kept a passport since I was twenty, renewed once and was now putting it to use. Constance Botello. I had not changed the name in the little blue book that showed no stamps.

I wasn't scared or even nervous. Amazing. This was by far the biggest adventure I had ever taken and yet, my deodorant was working just fine.

The man to my right had covered himself with a blanket and within ten minutes of takeoff, was snoring like a hungry pig. I had heard him speak to the Attendant as soon as we were seated asking not to be disturbed for dinner. Imagine, he was giving up a free meal. Resting my head against the window I tried to catch some sleep before eating.

The pasta was quite good, in spite of all I had heard about airline food. I downed another glass of wine, again red, and passed on dessert. After all, this Lady had to look svelte for the barrister.

The Barrister. What would he be like? Lofty, handsome, impeccably dressed in an office with British antiques centuries old. He would kiss the back of my hand on our meeting and offer me tea. I would sit on the Louis Fourteenth chair with perfect posture and request, no demand, further certification of my title. He would smile, open a small safe next to his desk and produce a diamond brooch with the crest of the Seated Title I had purchased.

And with the image of The Barrister pinning the brooch on my fake Chanel suit, I fell into a deep sleep.

Examining my custom forms and passport, the officer looked me intensely, straight in the eyes. "No business, just pleasure?"

"Yes, I'm here . . " I stopped to think for a moment. "I'm here purely to sightsee. You know, museums, restaurants, shopping, Windsor . . ." The Officer stopped me mid-sentence.

Waving me through the line, he handed me back my passport, "Welcome to England. Enjoy your visit."

Before walking away, I asked, "Where can I catch the train to London?"

The Officer responded. "After you go down the

passageway on your right, follow the signs to London Express or London Connect. Or, you may want to catch a cab or the Underground. Just follow the signs."

"Thank you. Ah. . ." I looked down, almost embarrassed to ask. "One last thing, sir." I raised my head. "Would you stamp it?" The mustached, uniformed man nodded his head and smiled broadly. I handed him back my blue little book and with the bang of a manual stamping machine, I became a world traveler.

I rolled my suitcase down the crowded hall and emerged into a huge open area with signs everywhere. According to my research, a cab would be at least one hundred American dollars. Best deal, the Underground which was in Terminal Three and very close to the Immigration area I had just exited. With the few pounds I had exchanged at LAX, I made my first British purchase and hopped the Piccadilly Line toward Cockfosters station, Earl's Court exit which was just around the corner from my hotel.

Time to think as the crowded train rushed toward London. On one hand, I was the determined woman who was going to show Rothstein that I was the real Lady who had befriended the Cookie Queen and the Brazilian billionaire's son. On the other, I was just a California girl pretending to be someone special in a world where titles, wealth and fame reigned.

CHAPTER TWENTY

The cool water felt great on my face and body. It took me a few minutes to figure out the European hand-held shower system but after accidentally spraying most of the bathroom, I became a pro. Hotel Indigo in Kensington was perfect. Old on the outside but new and clean once you entered the huge double glass doors. My beautiful room had a Queen bed, desk, flat screen television, WI FI and small refrigerator. Perfect.

Peter said I should fight the desire to go immediately to bed. This proved quite easy since the excitement of being in a foreign country trumped the exhaustion of the ten-hour flight and eight-hour time difference.

Refreshed, I was ready to take on London. First stop, The Blackbird, a quirky pub around the corner from the Indigo, suggested by the hotel doorman.

"What can I get you dearie?"

"Menu please."

"Cumin' up. What to drink?" The waitress sounded like she had been sampling the brew all afternoon.

"What do you recommend? A light beer maybe?" I had no idea.

"No light beer here. When in London, you drink the real stuff. How about some London Pride?"

I was embarrassed by my naiveté. "I'm sure you are very proud of your beer but I really don't know which to order."

"Dearie, that IS the name of the beer. One London Pride cumin' up."

I sat back and buried my face in the menu hoping the three men in the next booth hadn't heard my conversation with the server.

"Here ya go." She slammed the beer down on the wooden table. "And you'll be eating?"

"Chicken and mushroom pie with mash, please." I handed back the menu and checked my cell for messages.

From Peter: Email me as soon as you're settled in. Be careful.

From Antonio: Missing you already.

From Mary: Mr. Rothstein would like $12.98 for the pads and pens you took from the supply room.

Holy shit. How did he know I took a few things and threw them in my brief case? That office must be rigged with cameras.

I texted Peter: In a pub near the hotel having dinner. All is fine but almost got run over crossing the street. Do you know they drive on the wrong side? Of course, you do. Big day tomorrow. Will email you after I meet with the barrister. Ta Ta.

The decision of what to wear was easy. I put on my blue gabardine suit, tan heels and accessorized with a fake Gucci purse, faux pearl earrings and a matching necklace. Makeup done and hair perfectly coiffed, I headed out to claim my victory.

"21 Temple St." I treated myself to a cab. The poor driver. I kept asking what different buildings were as we drove the streets of London town.

He answered politely. "Earl's Court over there. This area is called Knightsbridge. Lovely shops. And of course, that is Harrod's." One amazing sight after the other. Everything seemed old but elegant, cosmopolitan but approachable. Stone facades and cobblestone walkways. "There's the Victoria and Albert Museum," the cabby offered. A few minutes later. "And there's Piccadilly Circus." From the glamorous neighborhood of Hyde Park, past Trafalgar Square, we arrived and stopped at a shop across from the old court house.

"Here you are Madam." The driver pulled over. "Eighteen pounds."

"I think you may have made a mistake. Are you sure this is 21 Temple?" I was starting to panic.

"Look at the address. This is 21. This is where you asked to go." He was not only persistent but correct.

I handed the driver a twenty-pound bill, exited the cab and stood in front of the business that looked like a British version of the American office supply store, Staples.

I hesitantly entered. "I'm looking for a barrister by the name of James Buckhold Stevens. I have this address for his office."

"Does he run a company called Elite Titles?" The man asked.

"Yes." I answered excitedly.

The shopkeeper pointed. "His postal box is over there. Third row from the top."

"What do you mean?" I was stunned. "There must be a mistake. Mr. Stevens is a lawyer. Here, I have proof. Is his office upstairs?" I pulled out all my documents with the address.

"People use our postal services for all kinds of businesses. We don't ask questions. We just supply them with a small box to receive mail. My apologies if this is a disappointment." The man seemed to be genuinely sorry.

"Can you give me a contact number for Mr. Stevens, or another address?"

The shop man shook his head. "No, that isn't possible. I'm sure you understand. Privacy."

I didn't understand. My chest felt tight. I had traveled six thousand miles to see a post office box?

"Do you by any chance have a telephone book?" I asked urgently.

Shop man gave me one. I flipped pages, checked and rechecked but there was no James Buckhold Stevens, Esq. listed.

I smiled and handed it back, quickly exiting the store. *This can't be happening. This can't be happening.* I walked in a daze for about ten blocks, through the Temple Bar area, under the Wren Gate until the point where my body caught up with my mind. I felt weak. *I'm so stupid. Stupid. Stupid.*

The sandwich shop I entered was quiet and provided the respite I desperately needed. It was before the lunch crowd and after breakfast. My body was trembling and mind searching for the 'whys'.

Over an untouched blueberry scone and coffee, I tried to put the pieces together. So many questions. Was the barrister running a scam? The land …did I own the land? I had proof that I did. Certified, documented proof. Where did the money go? Who signed the deed? Why had I been so gullible?

Through tears, I dialed Peter.

"What's wrong, Connie? You sound like hell. What time is it anyway? I was asleep."

"Ten in the morning here. I'm in a restaurant." My mouth was resting on the phone trying to get as clear a connection as possible. "Peter, it's a postal box. There's no office. I don't know if there's a real lawyer. It may all be fake."

I could hear Peter take a deep breath. "Oh sweetie, I'm so sorry. You must be devastated. Catch the next flight back? Come home."

"No." I blurted and then continued in a whisper. "I'm not ready. I need to sort things out. I'll stay a few days. See some sights. Eat London food. Soothe my wounds with lots of pie and crumpets. Come over, Peter. Be with me. Please."

Peter declined, saying he just couldn't leave the gallery but had me promise to check in with him every day.

I was on my own, feathers ruffled, fantasy crushed, defeated, deflated and thoroughly disgusted.

CHAPTER TWENTY-ONE

S trewn over the hotel bed were the vestiges of my Noble acquisition – deeds, legal papers with seals, pictures of family crests. No matter how I tried to be realistic and logical, a tiny part of me still wanted to believe my title was genuine. I read from the scroll: *Lady Stephanie Eugenie Parker Livingston du Exeter bestows upon the above subject one square foot of land from her estate, henceforth entitling said subject the seated title of Lady Constance of Widford.* I paid for the land, so I own the title.

Then it hit me. I needed to confront Lady Parker Livingston. I needed to see my land. It became so clear. I would go to Exeter, meet with the person who sold me the parcel, take pictures and prove my Noble status through British real estate. This quest now wasn't for Rothstein or Mary or Twibble. It was for me. I had dived into this project with the hopes of it changing my life, of giving me a new life. The story I created had been a lie, but my acquisition was real and I needed to prove it.

The hotel Concierge gave me directions. "Take a cab

to Paddington Station and then a train to Exeter. It will take you two, maybe three hours, depending on if you can catch an express or local. Beautiful countryside. Are you checking out?"

I thanked the helpful employee and said I would only be gone for the day. "I'd best hurry. Exeter awaits." I caught myself talking in a fake British accent.

By noon I was on an express to the small suburb of London. I bought a sightseeing book in the terminal and perused it while we zipped by old tenements, acres of industrial parks and finally, the beautiful countryside the Concierge had mentioned. It was 3:00 when we pulled in to the Exeter Central station. I would have just enough time to find the estate, talk to Lady Livingston, grab some pictures and make the eight o'clock train back to London. My mission was to conquer and redeem.

I hailed the first cabby I saw, jumped in and asked if he knew how to find a Lady Livingston's home. "It's a noble manor house. I'm sure it's quite famous."

"American?" the old driver asked.

"Yes, and I'm in a huge hurry. Is it far?"

"No, about ten minutes. Quite some place. You know the Lady?"

"Actually, we have a business association." I thought that was a perfect answer. "Real estate," I added.

In front of me was the most beautiful home I had ever seen. The tour book said it was built in 1833, Tudor Revival. There were two enormous wrought iron gates at the entrance that led to the main house. Surrounding the estate were acres of land, protected by high walls. The only thing missing were guards wearing red and black uniforms with shiny fringed epaulets and plumed hats guarding the palace.

No one was manning the gates. I couldn't find a doorbell. The only other person in sight was a photographer hopping around shooting the entrance from every angle possible.

"Excuse me. Hello. I don't mean to interrupt but do you have any idea how I can get in to speak to the owner?"

The man stopped and pointed toward an intercom box partially hidden by a bush. "Do you know Lady Livingston?" he asked.

"Not exactly." I walked to the intercom and buzzed, jumping back when someone answered almost immediately.

"Yes. May I help you?"

"I'd like to speak with the Lady of the house." I was matter of fact.

The box answered, "That is impossible unless you have an appointment. And, there are no appointments scheduled for this afternoon. Good Day."

I rang the buzzer again. The same gentleman answered and I spoke. "Please don't hang up. You see, I really need to get onto the property and take some pictures and talk to Lady Livingston. Just need to confirm something."

The box again answered, "Madam, please leave immediately."

I was furious. Again, I pushed the button. This time, no one answered. I was determined and decided to squeeze through the iron bars. One leg went through but even with the breast reduction, the girls couldn't make it.

The photographer stood nearby, witnessing my resolve. "You are a determined little bugger, aren't you?"

"Mind your own business. And stop staring at me." Rethinking the situation, "You know, you could be a gentleman and give me a hoist over the fence."

"Not on your life, madam. Watching you is absobloodylutely too much fun. As you said, I'm minding my own business."

Giving the photographer a nasty look, I surveyed my other options and decided to put my high school gymnastics class to good use. With difficulty, I shimmied up the fence post and grabbed onto one of the pointed pillars at the top. Now, all I had to do was drop down the other side but, I lingered too long. Sirens started to blare.

"Right. You probably shouldn't have done that." The man was now taking pictures of me. "Not sure where you hail from but in England, trespassing is illegal."

I was stuck at the top of the wall. I couldn't pull myself over and it was too high to jump back down. Three security guards swarmed the area in seconds and with a bull horn, demanded I get off the wall. "Come down immediately. The police have been summoned."

I yelled, "I would if I could." Meanwhile, a small tourist van pulled up to the gates and five Japanese men exited, cameras clicking. I was mortified as they stared and pointed.

Someone who looked like a gardener arrived in about five minutes hauling a tall ladder. Almost simultaneously, a police squad car squealed up to the gates, sirens screaming. It was chaos. The tourists kept clicking away, capturing every minute with their Nikons.

I used the ladder to climb down and saw a uniformed officer waiting. "What is going on?" I asked. "Watch it." I was being frisked. "Down on the ground." The officer demanded. "Put your hands behind you and spread your legs." I was horrified. It was a scene from every cop show I had ever watched. "I'm really just trying to speak to someone. I'm not a criminal. I'm not a thief. I'm an American who owns property here."

The officer spoke again. "Sure, you do. I advise you to be quiet and cooperate. Bloody right. You own property here like I'm the Queen's cousin."

Cuffs on, I was being arrested.

CHAPTER TWENTY-TWO

"May I ask who you are?" I was addressing a woman in a police uniform seated behind a small metal desk.

"I am the Local Policing Inspector Jane Bowles, assisting the Constable who leads the Beat Team who is managed by the Sergeant who heads the Neighborhood Division. Clear?"

The building had stone walls, few windows and low ceilings. I doubted anyone over six feet could stand without hitting their head on the beams. "No, nothing is clear." I honestly answered. "Can these cuffs come off?"

The formidable woman in a dark navy-blue uniform stood, dropped a screen in back of her desk and projected a picture of me on top of the gate. "Security camera took this. And your explanation?"

"Actually Officer…"

"Inspector." She corrected me. "I'm the Inspector."

"Sorry." I continued. "Actually Inspector, looking at

that picture you can't tell if I'm trying to get in or out. Can I make a phone call?"

"Of course. What number would you like?" The Inspector picked up her land line ready to dial.

How ingenious I became. "I'd like to speak to Barrister James Buckhold Stevens in London. I don't have his number with me. I'm really not dangerous. Could you please remove the cuffs?" They were really starting to hurt.

"In due time." The Inspector looked past me to the man standing in back. "Oswald, get the London number for Barrister Stevens." The arresting officer went into a back room and the Inspector continued looking at the little blue book that was taken from the travel wallet I wore around my neck. "Your passport says your name is Connie Botello?"

"Yes," I answered. "Although, I do have another name."

The Inspector became intrigued. "Do tell, Miss Botello. You have an alias?"

I squirmed in the seat. "No. Not exactly. You see, I own some property on the estate of Lady Parker Livingston which gives me the right to the Noble title of Lady Constance Widford."

The room became silent. I could almost hear the movement of the three officer's eyes looking from one to the other. And then, a huge burst of laughter.

I scanned the room. Why were they laughing at me? "What's so funny? I have all the papers. I paid a lot of money for my property. I have a deed. Proof."

The Inspector spoke. "Lester, remove her cuffs." Sitting down, she leaned on the desk and spoke quietly. "Miss Botello, I thought the name of your lawyer sounded familiar. Sadly, you have been used. It's a scam. Scotland Yard has been after whoever uses the nom de plume of Barrister Stevens for many months. Everyone here in Exeter has known about it. He's infamous all over England. Once you mentioned the land, I recognized the name. Sorry you made the long trip to England when actually last night he was caught emptying his postal box and arrested. If you want to see him, you'll find him in a London jail."

I sat in silence, my eyes tearing.

"Miss Botello," the Inspector continued, "Lady Livingston inherited her estate from her father and grandfather and a two-hundred-year line of Noble relatives before. She has not and will not be selling even an inch of her property. Oswald," she yelled, "forget about getting that number."

I felt shame to the point of not being able to look

anyone in the face. "May I leave?"

The Inspector rose. "Miss Botello, I empathize. One of my countrymen scammed you, but there still is the matter of your trespassing. I'm afraid I will have to pursue the charges and contact a representative for Lady Livingston to see how we will proceed. Please follow me to the holding cell."

"Jane, is that really necessary?" The handsome gate photographer had entered the station. "If you release Miss Botello into my custody, I'll keep an eye on her and make sure she doesn't bother Lady Livingston any further. How about it?"

The Inspector smiled. They were obviously friends. "This is highly unconventional but I do feel sorry for you Miss Botello. Do you promise to stay away from places you shouldn't be and definitely stop climbing walls on private property?"

"Yes, Inspector. I promise."

Inspector Jane turned to the photographer. "She's all yours. Anyway, I'll need the holding tank for tonight's rousers. Safe travels, Lady Constance. Consider this a noble gift."

CHAPTER TWENTY-THREE

"You swooped in like Cinderella's prince. Thank you ...I'm sorry, I don't know your name."

"Harry Parker. Gate photographer at your service." The pink cheeked Brit extended his hand.

I replied after a hardy shake. "How did you pull that off? With that police lady?"

"We've been neighbors for years. Exeter is a small place. There's University students, farmers, shop keepers, the pub owners, a few professionals. Locals all know each other."

"Well, I thank you for delivering me from the most embarrassing experience of my life. I should get to the station. Catching the eight o'clock back to London. Thank you, again."

"I'll see you off."

"That's not necessary." I wanted to get back to the hotel and shower off this entire ordeal.

"I insist. After all, you are in my custody."

"You're not one of those nuts Scotland Yard is looking for, are you?"

Harry laughed and raised his hands as if to surrender. "Quite. I confess. The parking ticket will be paid next week and The Yard will take me off their most wanted list."

His small Fiat was parked a block away. Talk came easily. Harry Parker took pictures of trees, oceans, animals, architecture … anything that was not human. Apparently, Lady Livingston's gates were new and Harry was officially the person who would preserve, in minute detail, what they looked like. Basically, the gate keeper.

"There are others, you know, who have fallen for that Noble title scheme. Don't be embarrassed. Anyway, moving on. Where are you from?"

He kept turning toward me as we talked. And my, oh my, he was easy to look at. His hair must have been blond as a child and now sandy brown. It was shaggy and in need of a trim. Cheek bones strong, eyes hazel, complexion on the light side and stubby beard. Maybe just shy of six feet tall.

"I'm from California. Near Palm Springs, about two hours east of L.A."

"I've heard of it. And you came to London because?"

"Well, it's a long story."

Harry jumped in. "Tell me. We only have time for the five-minute version."

"Well, I thought my life was a mess so I bought the square foot of land on the Livingston estate to get a Noble title, moved to L.A., worked in an art procurement business that exploited the Ladyship thing, which I admittedly loved, and got outed after I was in a car accident and my boss found out I had put down a phony address on my job application and bought my title." I ran out of air and took a deep breath. "I came here to redeem myself, Harry. Since I had a deed, I believed it might be for real. Stupid."

"And now what?"

"I'll go back to my old job in Palm Desert working at a gallery, California Desert Art. I'm small town Connie Botello, not worldly Lady Constance." A blanket of sadness came over me. It must have shown.

"Cheer up. You seem quite lovely, full of beans, Connie Botello. By the way, I've heard being a Noble isn't all it's cracked up to be." He smiled and continued. "I have a feeling this is your first trip to England, right?"

I nodded. "First trip out of the States."

"Then don't go home. Stay for a week or two and I'll

show you spectacular art, fabulous architecture and the most beautiful scenery in the world. I've lived here my whole life. I know it. I studied it. I'm a perfect guide."

"Why?" I asked.

"Because from the minute I saw your determination at the manor house, I knew you were someone I'd like to know. And you make me smile."

"As tempting as that sounds, Harry, I don't know you and traveling with a stranger is beyond crazy. Ever hear of stranger danger?"

Harry agreed. "Yes, I guess it would be quite mad. But on the other hand, life is about risks. You, of all people, know that."

He was convincing, noting that without him, I would still be in jail. In fact, he offered to turn around so I could get references from Jane, the Inspector, or anyone else I chose at the police station.

"I'll pay my own way." I wanted to set the ground rules.

"Noted. I would expect that. After all, I'm a photographer." Harry replied.

"Two rooms. No hanky panky. I have a boyfriend."

"And I a girlfriend, albeit she lives in South Africa."

"Strictly an information gathering experience. Like a

university class." I was adamant in my rules.

"I'm sure you can teach me a lot." Harry smiled.

I made the eight o'clock train by minutes. Plan was that Harry would meet me tomorrow late morning at the hotel. For three hours, as the train whizzed toward London, I questioned what I had just agreed to.

Maybe it would turn into a fling. Maybe I would just make a new friend.

A day of disappointment, adventure and meeting one hot tour guide.

Note to self: Buy pepper spray and a whistle first thing in the morning.

CHAPTER TWENTY-FOUR

I paid my bill and sat in the lobby speculating if Harry Parker would be a no show.

Peter was explosive on the phone the night before. *How can you travel with a stranger? Have you gone totally off your rocker?* But there I was, sitting on a red leather couch, pepper spray in my coat pocket, waiting for the man who kept me out of jail.

"You're very punctual, Mr. Parker." Dressed in jeans, a green plaid flannel shirt and low-cut tan boots, Mr. Photographer took my suitcase and escorted me out of the Indigo and to his waiting VW Tiguan.

"Where's the Fiat?" I asked.

"Oh, I borrowed the wagon. More room. Now, I have questions to ask before we take off. Mainly, how long can you stay in Britain? Can you give me a fortnight, two weeks?"

I was taken aback. "No. That's way too long. How about four days? Don't you have to work?"

Harry countered. "I'm freelance. Work can wait. I can't show you much of anything in four days. How about ten?"

I was bargaining. "A week. No more. But before we leave, I need to make sure you are clear about this arrangement. You have your room and I have mine. Understood?"

The gentleman was a gentleman and agreed. We shook and had a pact.

"Figure we'd go to Stonehenge today. After, we'll go over to Salisbury, a lovely little town and then on to Bath. How does that sound?"

I nodded. I had no idea what to expect and what there was to see. Harry continued. "I've made reservations at a charming B & B. You owe me one hundred fifty pounds but it includes a full breakfast."

"Sounds just ducky." I answered with my fake British accent. "But Harry, I have to watch my budget. I'm not a rich American, you know." I caught myself snickering. Of course, he didn't. He knew nothing about me except that I pretended to be someone I'm not.

The pictures you see of Stonehenge don't capture its enormity. Harry shared that when he was a youngster, he could climb and play on the rocks. Now, there was protective fencing surrounding the entire site.

"It dates back to 3000 B.C. Some say it was for

astronomical measurements. Others think it was ritualistic. All I know is that it's breathtaking." Harry stared at the immense stone pillars and archways. "I've photographed it at least 200 times and always see something different."

We arrived in Salsbury right before lunch. Harry bought fresh bread, three different cheeses, grapes and two bottles of bubbly water. We ate on a park bench then continued through the city passing streets named Ox Row, Oatmeal Row, Fish Row and Butchers Row.

"Thank you, Harry, for a lovely lunch, Dessert is on me."

"I'll hold you to that. Tell me more about yourself. Besides art, what are you keen on?"

"Movies and music." I responded as we walked the narrow streets, window shopped and strolled through The Close all the way to the cathedral.

"It's 404 feet tall." Harry shot photos while he talked. "Tallest spire in England. Thirteenth century. Blinding."

I craned my neck upwards and stared.

He continued. "Amazing, isn't it? Stand over there. I want you in the picture."

I looked at my personal guide and smiled. "I hate having my picture taken. But for you, Harry, snap away."

His ruddy cheeks and undeniable charm were getting to me.

"Put your hand on the pew and tilt your head just a bit to the left."

I felt awkward and must have looked like a stiff bird. Harry approached, cradled my head in his hands and gently positioned the pose. "There, you look smashing." His hands lingered on my face just long enough to give me a chill.

From Salisbury we headed to Bath, a one-and-a-half-hour drive. "And you, Harry, what is your passion besides photography? And how have you stayed single for …how old are you?"

Harry turned down the radio. "Thirty-five. I also love music, theatre, antiques and black and white movies. And no, I'm not gay. I have a huge obsession for race car driving and football, European, not American."

I wanted him to answer the being single question.

"And . . . ?"

Harry grinned. "Yes, the dating questions. I've been in a serious relationship a few times, but no one, including the South African, I've wanted to marry."

We laughed about binge watching old I Love Lucy reruns, especially loving the one in the candy factory and we played a telling game of Truth or Dare.

Harry: Who is the sexiest man on earth besides me?

Me: That's easy – George Clooney. What was your most embarrassing moment?

Harry: Definitely when I peed my knickers on the cricket field when I was twelve years old. Yours?

Me: On a turbulent plane ride. I peed all over myself in the lavatory.

Harry: I dare you to ask the next passerby for a shilling.

I crossed the street, slyly handed a young girl a coin and then loudly asked for it back. "Please, could you spare a shilling? The child quickly ran off with my money leaving Harry and me bent over in laughter.

"I saw what you did." Harry couldn't stop laughing. "Serves you right. My turn. I dare you to hop on one foot while singing a Beatles song at the next stop we make."

Next stop was a road side café. I ordered coconut custard pie. Harry ate mince. I jumped on one foot, sang Eleanor Rigby and made a complete spectacle of myself. I hadn't acted like such a child since, well, never.

It was just after sunset when the VW pulled up to the B & B. The sky still had a yellow glow at the horizon. Oldsfield House looked charming with its thatched roof and exposed beam exterior. As soon as I walked into the sitting room, any lingering fear about this adventure vanished. I felt safe, comfortable. The love seats were covered in navy and tan chintz with matching tufted chairs. The ceiling was high with drapes folding down past the chair rail and eighteen-inch base boards, pooling on the floor. The lobby smelled of freshly baked cookies. I had known Harry for twenty-four hours but it seemed like months.

Rooms secured and luggage stored, we drove into Bath.

"Now, if either of us were rich, we'd be staying at the Royal Crescent." Harry, with his ever-present camera around his neck, pointed to what looked like a castle. We stopped so he could take a few shots. It was the most opulent hotel I had ever seen, obviously getting its name from its shape. Harry continued. "Isn't it sumptuous? Built in the 18th century. We'll come back for a soak in the spa later."

"You said it was terribly expensive." I was calling him out.

"Yes. But I know someone." Harry winked, took my arm and slipped it through his so we were strolling arm in arm.

CHAPTER TWENTY-FIVE

"There has to be a place in the hotel I can buy a bathing suit." I said nervously.

"Nope. But the baths are private." Harry did his sexy wink.

"I'm not going in a hot tub naked with you Harry. We have a deal, remember?" My body image was still that of the chubby Italian.

Harry chuckled as we walked the stone hallway to our secluded room. "Constance, I'll turn around and when you're in, you to do the same. Come now. We're adults."

I came out of the changing room with a huge towel wrapped around my body covering me from shoulders to toes. Harry wore a small towel around his waist, just large enough to cover his private parts. Thank goodness, no camera around his neck.

He spoke. "Now I'm going to turn around and you get in."

The water felt wonderful. Soft. "I'm in." My voice echoed off the rock walls.

For the next forty minutes we relaxed in the steaming pool, talked and laughed. He stayed on his side and I hugged my corner. Harry had attended Exeter College, remained in the area to work for an advertising company, started his own business last year and was an only child.

His voice was soothing, like a minister or shrink. "These waters are known to be therapeutic. Healing. Fixes what's broken."

"What a kick. Are you suggesting I'm broken, Harry?"

"Don't take things so literally. And by the way, not beyond repair." He laughed and then cleared his throat. "I'm just getting to know you but there seems to be an underlying sadness in your tone. And, you are quite guarded. Maybe tomorrow we'll discuss this more. Anyway, it's time to go to the hotel. We have a busy morning in town before we head off to visit Shakespeare."

"Wait a minute, Mr. Psychologist. I'm a perfectly normal woman who just happened to be in an upsetting situation when we met."

Harry was quiet for a moment. "You are right. I apologize. We obviously have a lot more to learn about each other. And, that will be fun."

Backs were turned, towels grabbed and nary a

lascivious look as we exited the baths. Well, maybe one quick peek on my part.

Accommodations at Oldfield House were amazing. A feather down mattress caressed my body like a mother holding her child. The cool air from the open window and animal sounds from adjacent fields lulled me immediately into a deep, restorative sleep.

I was startled when my cell rang. "What." My voice was hoarse and low.

"Are you alright?" It was Best Friend. "I've been worried."

"I'm sleeping and I'm fine. Goodbye." I was annoyed.

Peter stopped me from hanging up. "Come on. Talk to me. I have big news. We've decided on the Ritz Carlton in Rancho Mirage for our wedding. Probably between Christmas and New Years. We have the 28th on hold. Expensive, but worth it."

I sat up, now fully awake. "Whoa. Wedding? So soon? Aren't you moving too quickly?"

"We're in love. Living together works. It's the next step. Be happy for me."

I was happy for Peter. My best friend getting married. I was also jealous. Peter continued, "And, I want you to give me away."

I swallowed hard. "Of course, Peter. I'll always be there for you, and Tony."

Changing the subject, Peter asked, "So, how's it going? You sleeping alone?"

"Yes, I have my own room. We're going to Stratford tomorrow and I need to get up early to finish sightseeing in Bath." We talked for another ten minutes until I could hardly keep my eyes open. "By the way, he's quite charming. Not rich like my Tony, but a devilish smile and so smart. He does this wink thing…"

"Go to sleep, my darling. Stay safe. Nighty night."

"Good night, Peter. Honest, there's no romance. A man and woman can be just friends. Look at us."

"Yeah, the Fairy and the Princess. Love ya."

CHAPTER TWENTY-SIX

Between Bath and Stratford, Harry told me about different photographic shows he had mounted. I shared my desire to have my own gallery one day. "Because of this Lady debacle, I'll be working again for my best friend in a studio he manages." I sighed. "It was nice while it lasted, but I have to face reality. Just don't know how to break it to Antonio. He thinks I'm Lady Constance. I really don't want to hurt him. Did I tell you he's the son of a Brazilian billionaire? I've been on his yacht. Amazing."

Harry listened as he drove. "No, you hadn't mentioned that. If it's a genuine all-consuming love, won't he accept the real you?"

"I'm not sure. Wouldn't blame him if he didn't trust me. I do like him. At least I like the idea of him. All-consuming love? I've never experienced that. God, I hate having to tell Antonio. There's no chance that I own the land? I honestly believed it was true."

"I'm absolutely sure, Constance. It was all left to Lady Livingston when her husband died a few years ago. That's public knowledge."

"Harry, do you know her?"

"Yes. Lovely woman," he answered. "Very philanthropic. We're almost in Stratford. First to Shakespeare's home or Anne Hathaway's cottage?"

"I loved her in Les Mis. Didn't know she lived here?"

Harry laughed. "Not that Anne Hathaway. It's the childhood home of William Shakespeare's wife. You know, Anne Hathaway."

Embarrassed, "Okay, I'm really coming off as an idiot."

Harry pulled the car over to the shoulder and turned off the engine. "Miss Botello, face it. You are neither a posh British Lady or an American idiot. You are a charming woman who seems to be floundering by not accepting the truth. You are being eaten up by a fantasy you bought in to."

"What a blunt thing to say, Harry. You see me as a fish out of water, don't you? A ditsy woman flittering around trying to be someone she isn't. I'm floundering?"

"A bit." Harry looked uncomfortable. "Sorry if that seemed unjustified but I've never met anyone so out of sorts with whom they are."

I opened the car door and bolted. Harry followed. "Are you off your trolley? Where are you going?"

"I don't know. I obviously don't know anything. Just leave me here and I'll thumb a ride back to London. Or will I get arrested for that, too?"

"Constance, stop. And yes, thumbing is illegal in Britain." Harry caught up, took off his gray nubby cardigan and wrapped it around my shoulders. "You're shaking."

My teeth were chattering. It was all catching up – the jet lag, the scam, the lies. I cried hysterically. "Oh God, I'm so lost."

Harry rocked me gently, rubbing my arms and stroking my hair. "Listen to me. You are not lost. You're in Stratford-On-Avon on a chilly November day, with a new friend who, lord only knows why, will take care of you while you're in England." Harry took a linen hanky from his jeans pocket and wiped my tears and continued. "You know, you can be a royal pain."

I snuggled a little closer and the Brit continued to talk. "Enough of this pity party. You messed up. We all have at some point."

"Not you, Harry." I blew my nose. "From what I see, you are perfection."

"Oh, you wouldn't believe some of the things I've done, especially at University. This chap, Wilbur, was supposed to sit an exam. I hated math and paid him twenty pounds to take the test for me. Well, instead, he went to the professor …"

Stratford-on-Avon was delightful. Lunch and a pint at The Swan, a visit to Shakespeare's birthplace, a side trip to Warwick Castle and a performance at the Royal Shakespeare Theatre filled the day and evening. I was exhausted and welcomed a good sleep at the small hotel Harry booked.

Day three took us to Liverpool and The Beatles Story. We drank coffee at The Casbah, where the phenomena of The Fab Four started and went to both McCartney's and Lennon's childhood homes.

Day four we headed South East along the A50 toward Leicester. Harry was excited and said he had a surprise, a special place in the countryside he wanted to stay before we went on to London. "It's on me. A birthday gift."

"My birthday was six weeks ago, Harry. What's going on?"

"There's this hotel, a country estate that brings back fond memories. I haven't been there for some time. It was my family's favorite place to weekend when I was young. Quite lovely and absolutely fit for a Lady."

"I'd love to see it, but remember, I'm paying my own

way."

"Not tonight, Constance." And then looking at me, "You have a difficult time accepting compliments, gifts, just about anything, don't you?"

He was right. Once, in sixth grade, Joey Pinsker gave me a silver ankle bracelet. He said he bought it with paper route money. After two days, I found Joey on Cedar Street and gave it back. Never understood why I didn't feel worthy of the anklet. Same with gifts from Peter. I didn't know how to accept.

Exiting the M50, we headed toward Melton Mowbray. Ten minutes later we pulled into a long driveway leading to a manor house called Stapleford. *Of all the hotels in Britain, how could we be here?* Stapleford, the estate I had found online and used as my fictitious families' home.

CHAPTER TWENTY-SEVEN

I didn't have the heart to tell Harry I was already familiar with Stapleford.

"Everything alright?" he asked.

"More than alright. It's magnificent. Feels like Lady Constance arrived home." We both laughed.

"Well, my Lady, for the next twenty-four hours, you will live your dream once again and be Lady Constance of Widford. Just let me check in at reception. Won't be but a minute."

Harry walked to the alcove desk as I wandered around the grand salon. Three guests dressed in traditional jodhpurs, helmet and cropped jackets were excitedly leaving for a hunt. Horses and barking hounds were waiting just outside the door. All I could think of was the poor fox.

"Here. I have the confirmation numbers. This is totally unacceptable." I heard Harry's raised voice from around the corner.

The flustered man replied. "I'm so sorry. Apologies. This never happens. Someone obviously double booked. I can offer you the Crabtree and Evelyn State room. Smashing space."

Harry motioned to the desk clerk to hold a minute and walked out of the alcove to where I pretended to be watching the riders mount.

"Constance, there is a slight problem. The hotel is overbooked. We can only stay the night if we share the Crabtree and Evelyn room or we could move on to another hotel."

I looked at Harry not sure if this was a ploy on his part or an honest mistake. "May we see the room?" I asked. "Maybe it has a large sofa."

As soon as the bellman opened the door, I knew the room was mine. It was like entering an arboretum with over 100 framed floral prints on the walls, flowered needlepoint pillows perfectly arranged on the four-poster bed with the fragrance of a luscious garden everywhere. The bathroom had a glorious tromp d'oeil on the ceiling and bowls of scented pedals on the counters and tub rim. It was a girl's dream. A Lady's dream.

"Could we have a minute, please." Harry asked the bellman to step outside and turned to me. "You will take the bed and I'll sleep …the couch is too short." Harry looked around. "I'll just sleep on the floor. I really want you to experience Stapleford."

I looked at Harry and smiled. He was trying so hard to be the gentleman.

"Look," he pleaded, "I know this isn't ideal, but by now, you know you can trust me."

Harry seemed to have all the qualities I admired and wanted in a man. He was smart, creative, kind, polite and quite pleasing to the eye. In fact, I found him very handsome, in a British country squire way.

He lived in England and I in California. Neither of us could afford a bi-continent relationship. It would never work. We were geographically unsuited. Latin God emailed and texted me every day saying he couldn't wait until I got back. That could work.

Would I trade a Billionaire's son for a man who drove a Fiat and perpetually had a camera around his neck?

"Pull," Harry shouted. "Now aim and shoot, Constance." We were in a field shooting skeet.

After maybe ten tries, I finally hit the disc. "I got it, I hit it. Harry, did you see that?" I turned and gave him a huge hug.

"Smashing. New rule. Every time one of us hits the

target, we hug. I quite liked the last one. My turn."

A dozen pulls, a dozen clay pigeons smattered. It became a big joke with hugs after every shot. Bear hugs, silly hugs, buddy hugs and then a hug that said *Let's be more than friends.* The wall I had put up was finally crumpling.

Two glasses of champagne at dinner, a Courvoisier chaser and my inhibitions vanished. We made love that night. It was sweet, delicious fulfilling love. Harry was tender with moves that made my toes curl and heart race. We kissed, caressed and moved with such determined passion that the four-poster bed shook. I finally knew what it was like to have unselfish, beautiful sex.

I woke at daybreak, slipped out of bed and from our bedroom window watched the sheep graze. On one side of the pane, the English countryside with its emerald grass and rolling hills. On the other, my beautiful English gentleman. Heaven, I thought.

"Come here, Lady Constance." Harry was awake. "Thank you for not making me sleep on the floor."

I laughed. "It was my pleasure, Mr. Parker. Our pleasure. Are you hungry?"

"For you." Harry grabbed my hand and pulled me back on the bed. Love making in the morning. Another new experience.

After a full English breakfast of eggs, bangers, crumpets, tomatoes, beans, jam and tea, we headed out to the stables. The extent of my equestrian experience consisted of a pony ride at a friend's birthday party when I was six.

"Smile." Harry yelled taking pictures as I mounted the gentle steed. "You look wicked on that horse. Just wicked."

We fed and brushed the Nubian goats, challenged each other at archery and walked hand in hand along the brook that ran through the estate. "My Dad and I would skip rocks here. Great man. You would have loved him."

"I'm sure."

"He was a lawyer, politician for the people."

I wanted to ask more about his family but saw he was someplace else, in a nostalgic reverie. We continued, mostly in silence, stopping only for tender kisses.

By late-afternoon, London was calling. I cherished my time at Stapleford. It was a perfect place for Lady Constance to have lived and loved.

CHAPTER TWENTY-EIGHT

Harry and I stayed in London five days. No more *you'll have your room and I'll have mine.* We closed that awkward gap between friends and lovers and became both.

Windsor, Tower of London, theatre…we toured all the usual sights.

At Harrods he bought me a hand painted Halcyon Days porcelain music box that depicted foppish men dancing in front of a Noblewoman seated on a throne. It would forever remind me of my own halcyon days.

"You know, Constance, I've become quite besotted with you."

We were outside Buckingham Palace waiting for the changing of the guard. Tears welled in my eyes. "Harry, I care about you very much, but I'm leaving tomorrow. My life is six thousand miles away. It's only been a little more than a week. Let's call this for what it was – a wonderful fling."

"A fling?" Harry raised his voice. "I never considered

it that. From the minute I saw you climbing over that wall in Exeter, I knew I wanted you in my life. I deemed it was more than a chance encounter. Obviously, these feelings are one sided. Sad you don't believe in love at first sight."

"Listen to me." I pulled away from the crowd for some privacy. "You have a girlfriend and I'm going back to Antonio and introduce him to the real Connie Botello. I don't know how he'll take it, if he'll dump me or what will happen. I need to find out. I owe it to myself and him." I leaned and kissed Harry on the forehead. "I do care about you, Harry." I couldn't believe I was the one being sensible "The past ten days have taught me so much. You're amazing."

"Then don't go, not yet." Harry pleaded.

"That's not fair. My home is in America. You don't understand."

"I'm trying to," he said in frustration. "Geographically challenged. For some mad reason, I thought we could figure this, whatever it is, out. Obviously, you don't think so." We walked quietly for several blocks. "Okay, go home, take care of things with the yacht fellow and come back. You can stay with me. There are art shops in Britain. I'll find you a job. Hell, we'll open a gallery together. Constance, I know this romance has happened with lightning speed but I'm giving you my heart. Take it. Please."

I was stunned and stood in silence. My stomach turned. I knew Harry liked me but his testament of caring was just short of saying the L word. No one had ever committed to me that strongly and I was afraid. "I don't know what to say."

Harry took a moment for my words to sink in, turned and gave me a hug. It wasn't a loving hug, more of a buddy pat on the back hug. "Your lack of words says it all. It's okay, Constance. We had a fling." He cleared his throat. "We'd best get back to the hotel so you can pack."

Harry's entire demeanor changed. He was now the guarded one.

Our time together had been magical and in an ideal world, we would have continued to date, marry and have three little British babies. Connie's world, my world, had never been even close to ideal. I felt a huge need to get back to familiarity, to Peter and the desert. I may have been running from commitment but also toward a new chapter in my life – a truthful chapter.

In the short time I had spent in England, Harry opened my eyes to so many things. He accepted my flaws, tantrums, insecurities. I began to accept them, too. He peeled away the onion to the real me and I began to recognize who I really was. I was naked in front of Harry. I was authentic and confident. And to my astonishment, I began to trust and like the person I was becoming.

As difficult as it was to leave this wonderful man, I was eager to get home and take back my life– Connie Botello's life. Commitment had to be put on hold.

We didn't make love that last night in England. Sleep wouldn't come. I tossed with frustration. In the morning Harry wanted to take me to Heathrow but I insisted on leaving the same way I arrived, via the Underground.

I had said many farewells but this was the most difficult.

"Harry, thank you. It isn't goodbye."

"Then what is it, Constance?"

"It's *I'll see you when I see you.* I'm going home to grow up."

And suddenly, all of Peter's lectures started to make sense. He wasn't trying to get me to be someone different, but wanted me to find myself. What Harry did in ten days Best Friend hadn't accomplished in years because of my blindness.

CHAPTER TWENTY-NINE

"Hi." Antonio called just as I moved slowly through customs. "The trip was wonderful. Yes, I'd love to have dinner. But I can't until next week. Maybe Thursday? Need a few days to catch up." I turned off my cell and wondered how it would be to see Antonio. Would I run into his arms and kiss him passionately? Romantic thoughts had to be put on hold. I had decisions to make.

Peter met me at LAX. It was time to just focus on Best Friend.

After a huge welcoming hug Peter said the words I needed to hear. "It's so good to see you. Missed you, darlin'. You doing okay?"

"I'm absolutely fine, Peter. I'm better than fine."

"How about the Brit. Hard leaving him?"

I cleared my throat and answered, "You have no idea how confused I am."

We talked nonstop the entire drive back to the desert. Peter caught me up on his wedding plans. I assured him that

I had come out of this mess a wiser and better person. "I have tons to do, Peter. But it's all good, all positive."

I packed up my Los Angeles apartment and hired two guys I found standing in front of Home Depot to load it into a rented U Haul. In Palm Desert, Peter, Tony, Bruce and Steven helped me unload. I was back in a one-bedroom flat Peter had arranged. The car leasing company graciously traded my BMW for a Prius, lowering my payments by half.

Everything was falling into place. The boys of BALS noticed my newly found confidence. Peter promoted me to assistant sales consultant which meant I would be in the gallery helping buyers with their purchases. My old job of cataloguing was filled by an enthusiastic young man who just graduated from an art school.

Lady Constance was not mentioned.

Harry did not email or call.

"I need this afternoon off, Peter. Going to see Antonio for the TALK."

"Back a few days and already asking for time off. Good thing you're friends with the boss." Peter jabbered as he hung a new Peter Max. "Good luck, sweetie. Que sera sera."

On the entire drive to Marina del Rey I practiced my speech. It would be direct but gentle. Honest. *Tony, I never meant to mislead you. I really did believe I had the title.* No. That wasn't the truth. *Tony, I had been insecure my entire life and I accidentally found a vehicle that would give me the cachet I needed to feel good about myself.* Bunk. I lied and had to fess up to Latin God.

So much traffic. I made it to L.A. in a little over four hours, instead of the usual two or three. And even with the traffic, I was early. Our plan was to meet at the marina taco stand at 7:00 PM. Unassuming, casual Antonio. It was 5:45 so I decided to see if the art had been delivered to the yacht and hung.

There it was, the massive white fiberglass floating hotel that led me to Antonio. It looked beautiful, glistening, twinkling in the water.

No one was on the aft deck. I took off my heels and walked up the winding stairs. Still no one in sight, so I proceeded into the main salon.

"May I help you?" A distinguished gray-haired man around sixty-five was seated on a couch watching television, feet up, cigarette in hand.

"Yes, I'm here to see Antonio Safra. I'm a bit early." I was uncomfortable and my voice became timid.

The gentleman got up and extended his hand. "I'm

Estefan Safra. And you are?"

I paused. "My name is Connie Botello. Pleased to finally meet you, Mr. Safra. I'm looking for your son. We have dinner plans."

Safra chuckled as he returned to the couch. "That's very interesting, Miss Botello, since I only have daughters. Three."

My heart felt like it was beating 200 times a minute. Shaking my head in disbelief, I continued. "No, Mr. Safra. Antonio, Tony. Dark haired. He told me…" Everything morphed in to slow motion as Latin God entered the salon carrying a glass of wine on a tray. I pointed. "That's him! Antonio!"

I don't know who was more shocked. Our words collided.

Mr. Safra: That's one of my deck hands, not my son.

Antonio: Lady Constance, what are you doing here?

Me: He's a deck hand?

Antonio dropped the glass of red wine on the tan swivel chair next to the couch. Mr. Safra's eyes widened as he shouted, "You're Lady Constance? Who's Botello?"

"I can explain everything, Mr. Safra. Honest. First, please give me a minute with Antonio privately. Please." I implored.

Safra threw his hands in the air and got up. "Antonio, you have thirty minutes to pack and get off my yacht. How dare you say you are a Safra. Only a Safra is a Safra! And you, young lady, figure out who the hell you are."

We were alone. Antonio started to speak but I interrupted. "I'm not Lady Constance. My family isn't British. I bought the title thinking it was real. I was fired from my job, turned in my leased BMW and I'm poor."

Antonio finally spoke. "You're poor?"

I began to laugh hysterically, so hard I could barely speak. "From all that you only got that I don't have money?" I walked to the bar and poured myself a glass of water. "You realize we both used each other. You wanted to climb the social ladder with a woman you thought was rich and I wanted to be loved. The fact that you claimed to be a billionaire's son was icing on the cake, cherry on the sundae. We both wanted to be rescued from our lives. How pathetic."

"You wanted me for my money. Yes?" Antonio yelled.

"Partially. A little. Yes, I was impressed with the yacht. But I really liked you and thought you liked me. You only wanted me for what the fake title represented." I was now bitterly angry. "You were using me, Antonio. I came here to come clean. I was also complicit but I couldn't live with myself pretending to be someone I'm not. I wanted to own up. I wanted to tell you the truth and prayed you'd accept me for who I am. To think I cared about you, that I thought I was actually in love. Only difference between us is that I learned my lesson." I paused. "I hope you learn yours, Antonio. Adios."

CHAPTER THIRTY

I was drunk. Peter and the boys were helping me unpack the last boxes. My cadence was like a Marine song. "One, two unwrap a shoe, three, four drink some more." I took a huge gulp of beer. "Unwrap a glass…" I stopped to think what rhymed. "…fall on your ass. I'm a poet. Not bad, huh?"

Tony chimed in, "Honey, that's beer talk, not poetry."

"You know guys, he wasn't even a good lay. Wham bam." My words slurred. "And then there was Harry. In bed, a genius. A fucking Einstein. You know, he hasn't called me once. I miss him and his huge …"

Peter interrupted me. "TMI, my dear. There are some things that really are sacred."

"I was going to say camera, Peter. You have a filthy mind but I love it."

Tony steadied me as I moved to the kitchen table. "I think it's time for bed, sweetness. We can finish unpacking tomorrow. Peter, help me get her in the other room."

I had started drinking around 10:00 in the morning and

continued all day. My mother said Sunday was a day of repentance. This one was for numbing misadventures.

Peter lifted the covers and I dropped to the mattress in a lump. "Antonio didn't want Connie. He loved that other woman. That imposter. I made her up and now she's dead. Adios Lady Constance. I hate Brazil and boats and Beverly Hills…"

Stroking my head, Best Friend consoled me as I drifted off to oblivion.

Weeks passed. Season was in full swing and business at the gallery was booming. I loved talking art with the customers. Peter and Tony confirmed December 28th as their wedding date. It was coming up fast. Steven and Bruce planned a poolside shower that promised to be over-the-top fabulous. I started to work on my Maid of Honor toast. *To my best friend. You have been my rock, my family. I wish you and Tony a lifetime of love and* … It needed work. Thanksgiving came and went. Christmas was quickly approaching. Life was moving forward.

And no contact from Harry. Many times, I thought of calling. But between the realization that we lived six thousand miles apart and neither of us had the resources to commute between continents, plus my insecurities of allowing someone to really care about me, kept me away from the phone and living with a broken heart.

"I don't believe it." Peter put down the phone just as a customer entered the gallery. "No, so sorry, it's closing time." He shooed the poor man out like a flustered woman herding chickens. It was only three in the afternoon. "Please come back tomorrow. Thank you. Again, sorry."

On Peter's asking, I locked the front door and questioned what was going on. It wasn't like Peter to turn a customer away, no matter how inconvenient. "Okay, what's up? Who was on the phone?"

Peter sat on the gray sofa and stared straight forward with a look of disbelief. "It was Taubman. He sold the gallery. It's gone."

"No." I was now in disbelief. "This gallery? Oh my God. Who did he sell it to? Why? Our jobs. Are we out of work?" The questions came flying out.

Peter said he was assured our positions were secure. No changes. Everything would stay as is except for the ownership. "The new owner will be in town tomorrow and requested a staff meeting at 2:00. I have no idea who it is. I was so flustered I didn't ask."

Art student stock boy went home. Peter and I stayed

behind trying to figure out why Mr. Taubman, the longtime owner, suddenly was getting rid of his business. "If he's ill," I said, "we would have known. Maybe he needs money or is getting a divorce."

"Maybe he's in trouble with the law? Or owes back taxes," Peter added.

We went over every possible situation until it became a joke. The bottle of Dom we kept in the refrigerator for big sales was making us giddy. "Maybe he wanted to turn the space in to a strip club but the city wouldn't give him a permit. Maybe he's running off with a male model to Ibiza and needs cash to support his new lover." We had to laugh or we might cry. The gallery wasn't only our bread and butter but a major part of our lives. For years it had been our heart and soul, our pride.

"It's not fair, Peter. Just as I get comfortable with my life, life screws me over."

"Connie, talk about screwing, have you heard from that English guy, Harry?"

"No. Not a word. The fling has flung."

"Email him or ..."

I interrupted. "Don't utter his name again. We have enough on our plates – your shower, the wedding and now, our jobs."

I couldn't talk about Harry. If I did, the flood gate of tears and disappointment would open. I missed him with all my heart and wondered if this unfamiliar longing that I was experiencing was real love.

✳✳✳

"Peter, you've gone to the bathroom four times in the past fifteen minutes. You okay?"

It was almost 2:00. "I pee a lot when I'm nervous. What if he…"

I interrupted, "Or she."

"What if he or she really hates art and it's just a money deal? An owner needs to be passionate. Damn, I wish I could have bought the place. Didn't know Taubman wanted to sell."

"Relax, Peter. Would Wayne Dyer say Que sera, sera?"

My back was to the door as I tried to soothe Best Friend. "Excuse me, I'm looking for Connie Botello." As soon as I heard the voice, I gasped and turned. It was him. A dream? A hallucination? No, it was real.

"I'm Connie Botello." I said coyishly, my heart racing.

He winked. That devilish, sexy wink I had grown to

love. "My name is Harry Parker Livingston, your new boss." He slowly walked across the room and stood so close I could feel his breath. "I rescued a young damsel in distress and then fell madly in love with her. You, Connie Botello, were that damsel and you are the one that stole my heart."

So many questions. But they would have to wait. I was in disbelief until …

That moment, that kiss. Then everything was real.

I pulled away from our embrace just long enough to say, "Harry, meet Peter. Best Friend, meet the man I absolutely love."

EPILOGUE

Six Months Later

Mary opened the mail that had just been delivered. Bills, advertisements, the usual invitations to gallery exhibitions.

And then she screamed. "Mr. Rothstein, Juliet, my God. Come here, now."

Rothstein ran into the reception area smoking his ever-present cigar followed by his dog. "A fire? What? Everything okay?" Realizing there was no immediate emergency, he continued. "Hell, Mary, is this about another free coupon for a blintz at Nate N Al's? I'm getting tired of your nonsense. Get back to work."

Twibble yelled as she entered the lobby. "If you so much as bother me again with your foolish, trivial …."

Mary waved the gold embossed piece of mail. "You're not going to believe this. It's amazing. Unbelievable!" The three leaned in to read:

Lady Stephanie Parker Livingston of Exeter, England
Joyfully announces the engagement of her son
Lord Harry Parker Livingston
To
Constance Botello of Palm Desert, California

When I met Harry, I had no idea he was nobility. I fell in love with a darling, red cheeked photographer with a beautiful heart and understanding soul. When Harry met me, I was a broken woman searching for her identity. Harry gave me love, understanding, confidence and the most important title of my life. I became his wife.

And that, my friends, is how I became a Lady – for real!

ABOUT THE AUTHOR

Sherry Halperin was born and raised in Beacon, New York. As a teen, she studied at the Dramatic Workshop in New York City and spent five summers at Cecilwood Theatre in Fishkill, New York as a summer stock apprentice and Equity Stage Manager alongside such notables as Barbra Streisand, Dustin Hoffman and Peter Fonda. She went west for College and received her degree from the Pasadena Playhouse College of Theatre Arts with a major in directing.

Ms. Halperin has consistently worked on projects in the arts from distributing feature films, agenting actors, directing stage productions and working on hundreds of hours of network and cable television as a writer, producer and director. Sherry wrote Domingo, an ABC children's series, for three seasons and went on to work with Dick Clark and Norman Lear. A few years back she produced world music concerts and ballets all over the United States in venues such as Lincoln Center and UCLA's Royce Hall.

Her last book, *Recue Me, He's Wearing A Moose Hat*, published by Seal Press/Perseus, has garnered praise from The London Times, Chicago Tribune and Newsweek, among scores of other print media. It has appeared on several best seller lists and was optioned for a feature film by Oscar nominee writer/director Frank Darabont.

Sherry continued to be active in film and television working on the award-winning feature film, Adopt A Sailor (as a producer starring Bebe Neuwirth, Peter Coyote and Ethan Peck). The film can currently be seen on Amazon Prime. Upon completing Sailor, she mounted two talk shows for the CBS affiliate in Palm Springs.

She is a past President of Women In Film and Television, was the 2011 recipient of the National Pen Women's Award for Performing Arts and received a U.S. Congressional Recognition for her contributions to the arts.

Sherry resides in Santa Cruz, CA with her six-pound poodle, Clouseau, has two married sons, two grandsons, writes daily, plays ukulele and piano daily and loves to cruise. As a humorist who strongly believes in the power of laughter to heal, enhance and empower a fulfilling life, her passion is to make people smile.